THE UNMAKING OF AMERICANS

The Unmaking of Americans:
7 Lives

MEL FREILICHER

SD
CWP

SAN DIEGO
CITY WORKS
PRESS

Copyright © 2007 San Diego City Works Press

All rights reserved. The author retains the copyright to this book. No part of this book may be reproduced in any form without written permission from the publisher and/or the author.

Every effort has been made to trace the ownership of all copyrighted material and to secure permission from the copyright holders. In the event of any question arising as to the use of any material, we regret the inadvertent error and will be happy to make the necessary correction in future printings.

ISBN 978-0-9765801-6-4
Library of Congress Control Number: 2007921271

San Diego City Works Press is a non-profit press, funded by local writers and friends of the arts, committed to the publication of fiction, poetry, creative nonfiction, and art by members of the San Diego City College community and the community at large. For more about San Diego City Works Press please visit our website at www.cityworkspress.org.

San Diego City Works Press is extremely indebted to the American Federation of Teachers, Local 1931, without whose generous contribution and commitment to the arts this book would not be possible.

Cover Design: Rondi Vasquez & Joe Keenan
Production Editor: Will Dalrymple

Published in the United States by San Diego City Works Press, California
Printed in the United States of America

Acknowledgments

Book 1 was published as a chapbook by Obscure Publications, 2003. "A Literary Li(f)e" was first published in poetic inhalation, *2005.*

Thanks to Stephen-Paul Martin for his insightful reading of the manuscript.

This book is for Joe.

Book 1
SMASHED AND SMASHING ICONS

***DOROTHY DANDRIDGE*: A Biography**
Donald Bogle
Amistad Press, 1997

***THE REAL BETTIE PAGE*: The Truth about the Queen of the Pinups**
Richard Foster
Carol Publishing Group, 1998

***WONDER BREAD AND ECSTACY*: The Life and Death of Joey Stefano**
Charles Isherwood
Alyson Publications, 1996

1.
DOROTHY'S DISAPPEARING DUST COVER

Dorothy Dandridge—like Marilyn Monroe and Liz Taylor—was a sizzling, dream goddess of the fifties. All audiences ever had to do was take one look at her—in a nightclub, on television, or in the movies—and they were hooked. She was unforgettable, Hollywood's first full-fledged African American star.
Although she worked tirelessly to climb the ladder,

          no room at the top,
          Dorothy became a dramatic actress unable to secure dramatic roles.

    most dazzling and sensational nightclub performers around, integrating some of America's hottest venues.
    But movie stardom was her dream.
                    an Academy Award nomination as Best Actress for her lead role in Otto Preminger's *Carmen Jones*.
                                  cultural icon

    As her personal frustrations grew,
at the age of 42, struggling with bankruptcy and alcoholism, Dorothy was found dead of an overdose of anti-depressant pills.

2.
FACTS OF LIFE

- Dorothy's mother, Ruby, was a comedienne and actress, a scrappy worker who ended her career on tv, as a maid in the series, "The Father of the Bride," and the neighbor Oriole in "Beulah." Ruby pushed Dorothy and her sister Vivian on stage. By the time she reached her teens in the Depression, Dorothy was working in such movies as "Going Places" with Louis Armstrong, and appearing at New York's Cotton Club in a trio called the Dandridge sisters.

  Ruby has been described as "not giving a damn about those kids," and she consistently refused to let them have any contact with their father. The girls were instructed to call Ruby's live-in lover, "Ma-Ma." A merciless disciplinarian, "Ma-Ma" would rip off Dorothy's underwear and examine her vaginally to determine if she was pregnant.

- Dorothy's only child, Lynn, was born retarded. The father was Dorothy's first husband, the talented black dancer Harold Nicholas. He was a philanderer, especially after they moved to Hollywood.

- The more successful Dorothy became, the more removed she was from available black men. Her lovers were stars like Peter Lawford, Frederick March, screenwriter Abby Mann (*Judgment at Nuremberg*), and, of course the highly influential Otto Preminger, who bought and furnished for her a French Regency mansion in Beverly Hills, when they were making *Carmen Jones* (she still had hopes that he would leave his wife). Five years later, a distant Preminger directed her in *Porgy and Bess*. He was acerbic about Jack Denison, her soon-to-be second husband, a sleazy character who owned a supper club in which Dorothy unhappily performed, and where she lost all her money.

- Preminger played a similar role, on a more magnificent scale, to an earlier lover, Dorothy's arranger Phil Moore, who engineered her nightclub career. Moore's material enhanced Dorothy's assets and stayed clear of her vocal limitations: he took care of grooming, styling and imaging.

Moore's career went on to span six decades, during which he did special arrangements for a galaxy of stars, including Lena Horne, Mae West, Ethel Waters, Ava Gardner, Frank Sinatra, Louis Armstrong, Marilyn Monroe, Lucille Ball, Ann Sothern, Count Basie, Dinah Washington, Charles Mingus, and later Diahann Carroll, the Supremes and Johnny Mathis. Dorothy was his favorite. In those days, Moore was never permitted to work with white female performers without supervision. "Judy Garland was always accompanied by a chaperon," he said. "No way a black guy could be alone with her in a rehearsal bungalow."

3.
CORRESPONDENCES OF THE FLESH:
The Soul Emerges (Briefly, for a Photo Op)

What happens is tragedy and melodrama. *When you fall, you cannot always stop.* Only a few ways of exiting with any dignity or aplomb, and possibly even with the means to attack (attract) intact.

Is it any wonder that Joey Stefano, hot hot hustler and porn star, was found dead at age 26, in 1994. That not-so-rhetorical question was recently posed by Peripatetic Book-Reviewer, pining for fleshy correspondences. This man does not wish to focus attention upon himself, or so he claims.

The mythic '50s pinup queen, Bettie Page, had characteristic black bangs: wholesome, voluptuous; bondage photos strictly with other women; *the disappearance*; "her decade long isolation behind asylum walls." Bettie stabbed and stabbed the defenseless old lady: bloodied house mate, furnished by a non-profit agency to assist the elderly.

As children, juicy Joey and bondage Bettie were both sexually abused by their fathers. Bettie's father traded dimes for the cowboy movies for her silence. *Joey's irresistible striptease.* He took drugs the way other people put on sunglasses when they go outdoors: as an automatic reflex.

Their steep, steep decline: notwithstanding Dorothy's Rice-a-roni tv commercial, and Bettie's fateful rendezvous with Billy Graham. When

Dorothy went bankrupt, she owed 77 creditors, and was involved in 8 different lawsuits. Secluded in her apartment, disoriented and depressed, Dorothy had late night "telephonitis." "She used to sing on the phone to my mother for two or three hours. I could take a shower and come back and she'd still be singing."

The motel on Hollywood Boulevard and La Brea Avenue where Joey was found slumped, needles in both arms. "Once in the early hours of the morning a panicky Dorothy phoned and asked Joel to come over immediately. Someone had taken the broiler out of her kitchen." (*When he arrived, the broiler was still on the kitchen stove.*) Bettie brandished a large kitchen knife while ordering her stepchildren to pray to the picture of Jesus. "If you take your eyes off this picture, I'll cut your guts out," she threatened. *(Could that be what they had recently taught her at Bible college?)*

Some kind of fleshy fatalism honestly haunts all us readers and weepers, even Peripatetic One, who likes to think of himself as hard-boiled, if not pickled, and whose function is decidedly ambiguous: trying to reflect judiciously on other lives while not calling attention to his own history or role as reflexive reflector. While some (whom P B-R could but won't name) have accused him of false modesty or worse, and fully acknowledging his own heaping solipsism, P B-R nevertheless denies all charges. Surely, even the most unkind critic would grant P B-R's genuine concern with America's internalized legacy of doom, specially dished out to non-rich, non-white: love it and hate it, U.S.A.

4.
THE FARM DEMANDED HARD WORK AND SO DID THE PORN MILLS

Bettie fetched water from a faraway well, watered crops, and picked rocks out of the soil so it could be seeded and plowed. Despite the poverty that forced Bettie and her siblings to walk to school without shoes on their feet, farm life had many advantages. On warm afternoons after lunch, she and her brothers and sisters ditched school to splash in creeks, and make up games. They were a lot happier than before, when the family had been shuffling through small dustbowl towns of Texas and Oklahoma. That ended in 1930, when their father Roy, a decorated World War 1 veteran, couldn't find a job as an auto mechanic, and stole a car to take his family to his mother's place in Nashville. After Roy was paroled from prison the next year, the family scraped together a little money to buy a 48-acre farm outside of Nashville. The marriage soon fell apart: more interested in carnal pursuits than farm life, Roy got caught rolling in the hay—literally—with a fifteen-year-old neighbor girl.

Bettie became very introverted, perhaps in reaction to her childhood abuse. But she was editor of the high school newspaper and yearbook, and avidly pursued the valedictorian's scholarship to prestigious Vanderbilt University. Accumulating a 97.19 g.p.a.—the valedictorian's was less than one-quarter of a point higher—Bettie would have graduated first, except she skipped a 2 hour art lab to rehearse for the senior play. Her yearbook declared that in 30 years hence Bettie would be likely to star in a remake of *Ninotchka*, with Mickey Rooney. On June 6, 1940, delivering her salutatorian's address, "Looking Forward," at the Nashville War Memorial auditorium, Bettie received a scholarship from the Daughters of the American Revolution to nearby George Peabody School for Teachers.

Her mother hadn't bothered to attend the graduation.

Life on the dance circuit was not an easy one. It meant long stretches away from home, adjusting to a new city every week, living out of a duffel bag (no suitcase necessary; leather straps don't wrinkle), wrangling with club owners over fees, killing time in unfamiliar places. Says one dancer who worked the circuit: "Clubs will do anything for you to make you happy—get anything for you. It's a pharmacy. You can get drugs from the owners, the managers, the customers, the other performers. Every single club has their house drug dealers."

Stefano's drug taking reached super-human levels: that does not constitute an anecdote. The PCP or angel dust habit, which he acquired when he left his middle-class, suburban home at 14, disgusted his friends when Joey moved into various of their upscale, West Hollywood apartment complexes (one known as the Porn Palace): he switched to trendy ecstacy and ketamine, or Special K, an animal tranquilizer which induced apparently highly desirable, catatonic "k-hole" states. Later, Joey preferred heroin.

His sexual appetites were every bit as insatiable. When he wasn't being paid for it, Joey could be found cruising the bars and bookstores; he would spend $200 a night on the 976 phone sex lines. Joey never had safe sex, and he was always sharing needles, so his HIV+ status came as no surprise. Still, he would be unable to continue working in the porn industry if it were made public, even though the majority of co-stars were in his same situation.

The porn mills demanded hard work: *Joey fetched water from the faraway well.*

5.
MORE FACTS OF LIFE

Dorothy's continuing studies at the Actors Lab were most important to her. Among her classmates were Charles Chaplin, Jr. and "a young blond named Marilyn Monroe, with whom Dorothy struck up a friendship." Located behind Schwab's drugstore at Sunset and Laurel, the Lab had been founded by some of America's most respected actors, including former members of the Group Theater in New York. Instructors included, at various times, Morris Carnovsky and his wife the actress Phoebe Brand, Hume Cronyn, Aline MacMahon, Sam Levene and Anthony Quinn. One of its administrators, who also studied and directed there, later became known as Joe Papp.

The Lab's interracial mix and liberal politics were viewed suspiciously by Hollywood's older, conservative generation. By 1948, the Tenney Committee, which had been established as California's arm of the House Committee on UnAmerican Activities, went so far as to label it a communist front. That year, the Lab held a Labor Day fundraising picnic in their parking lot, which provided an opportunity for its patrons to meet and mix with the staff. Planned for the day was a program of skits, songs, along with other activities, food stalls and a bazaar. At one point, Anthony Quinn asked Dorothy to dance; blacks danced with whites (actually, Quinn was half-Mexican). A particularly vicious Hollywood gossip columnist predictably termed the whole event, "pretty partylinish."

Hedda Hopper, who everyone in Hollywood knew was a rabid, ultra-conservative, declaimed in the *Los Angeles Times*:

(*VOICE OF HEDDA HOPPER*:)

...Out of Character. The Actors Lab made no friends when they gave an open-air barbecue, which included dancing between Whites and Negroes. They used a parking lot on Sunset Blvd for their dancing space where one and all could see. This group's corny idea of being liberal will eventually lead them into trouble. The situation has nothing whatever to do with racial prejudice or discrimination; every man in the world is as good as he is in his heart, regardless of race, creed or color. But that doesn't mean they have to intermix. Right or wrong, the great balance of the community has this deep-rooted conviction, and they were shocked at this display by the Actors Lab. That's the sort of thing that leads to race riots.

6.
BATHING BEAUTIES (A)BOUND

Hedda Hopper flounces into the chic club Copango on the arm of her latest, bouncing boy toy—hot baby, luscious flesh, juicy juicy Joey Stefano. "MORE THICK PLOT," a beguiled yet only slightly bemused Desi Arnaz groupie gaily cries, while beauteous Joey bares his bountiful buns right there on the glittering dance floor. "Who is that queen with the big butt and so much attitude?" inquires one perplexed patron.

Like J. Edgar Hoover, a veritable Flamenco floozie currently kicking up her hoary heels to "The Hustle," heartless Hedda Hopper knows absolutely everything about utterly everyone. She creams in her own dossiers; Ginger Rogers' fascist mom dementedly adds the vitriol. Meanwhile, rapacious Roy Cohn shakes (it) vigorously before pissing bile. It's definitely Slap-Happy Hour! (Peripatetic Book-Reviewers everywhere, beware!)

This season's biannual Blue Chip Ball is being held at Club Mocambo (momentarily renamed) where Dorothy is appearing as temporary replacement for Desi's usual singer; as a result, she will soon land a gig in Las Vegas' prestigious Club Bingo, where her friends Nat "King" Cole and Sammy Davis, Jr. have already performed. They were permitted to be in the lounge *only* when they were performing. Under no circumstances were they to socialize with any of the patrons, or dine at the club.

Joey is restless, feckless and fey on the disco dance floor, GRAVITY'S TOMORROW: there, he prowls through time for horny hustlers like himself. Joey prefers them beefy, bruising and hairy and oh-so-chewable: otherwise, he could've gone for daring Daddy Desi himself in a big, big way. (Quite a would-be treat for the virile young Anthony Quinn!)

"Get your cocks hard!" Joey callously commands fellow porn stars on torrid set of *Tijuana Toilet Trash*, imperious yet somehow twinkling. They must needs oblige him.

Joey is a tantalizing doll, a proud and aggressive, bottomless bottom: a new kind of porn star, in a macho world dominated by muscular, studly tops who unblinkingly eschew cock-sucking, and all visible signs of desire, even their own narcissistic imperative to be worshipped. This is Joey's provocatively lewd, thrillingly lascivious, big-buns triumph—his and Chi Chi La Rue's, maverick drag queen entrepreneur who produced and adored Joey, defying the established porn studios' so-called wisdom. Together, they ate mucho Twinkies, delivered fresh from Pink Dot. But it didn't show on Joey, at least not in a tawdry disco glow where Brandy is left to toot her own damn horn.

When repugnant Roy Cohn flashes wads of bills before glazed eyes, Joey is too stoned to recognize the face of evil: "ugly" still registers rapidly, though Joey's been hooked on heroin since age 14. It's an open secret that both men are HIV+—you can just tell that Cohn expects some definitive bareback action later. Meanwhile, Bettie has tried to fly out of her third-story, New York apartment window—a prelude to later, full-blown paranoid schizophrenia. Hedda frugs and hops heartily, licking the crusty lid off joyous J. Edgar's tipped and tinted tits. (Both celebs are positively well-known for wearing an evening gown like nobody's business.)

Dorothy—infinitely shy, remote and glamorous, tipsy—nevertheless defends herself with the strategic ferocity of a Cold War cutie about to cash in. After intensive consultation with politically experienced friends, she issues a statement, pointing out that she has been asked to make numerous appearances by many organizations, such as Catholic Youth Organization, B'nai B'rith Brotherhood Week, Red Cross, Cerebral Palsy, Heart Campaign. Although she agrees to answer any questions which MGM might put to her, Dorothy refuses to sign a loyalty oath.

About the Actors Lab, Dorothy says, "This was one of the few outlets available to a young actress of my race seeking actual workshop training. Attending the lab was in direct relationship with my theatrical ambition." An avowal that she was never affiliated with the Communist Party or any of its front organizations closes with, "I have at no time been politically active. My sole interests are towards having a successful career and aiding my people."

Much later, after the dance, these 3 beauties are in an amusing melee together. (All take or *are* booty beauties.) It happens in Delmonico's back rooms, where there's a huge pool, medium-sized one, and a hot shower. Democratically, Joey jumps into the large body of water, and cocks an inviting eye. Across a crowded room, Bettie and Dorothy exchange a fleeting, slightly weary, very knowing smile, then move on to lower and upper decks respectively. Bettie had already been posing in swimwear that day; deciding this is too much like work, she sighs for the duration. Dorothy definitely regrets everything, nothing (*rien*).

The dizzying disco dancing is dazzling; drugs flow like a rose-colored fountain in heat. Just as Joey is slipping out of his bathing, and into his glorious birthday suit, hatted and harried Hedda Hopper comes hobbling along, stumbling, searching for her ostensible boy-toy escort—though she always makes a big production of not sleeping with Joey, or anyone else "out of wedlock." On the verge of letting loose with vicious invective, luckily Hedda observes that lust-crazed Cohn is one of several unappetizing denizens of Delmonico's back room intently peering into Joey's nether regions. Needing Cohn to butter her toast all right, Hedda vaguely attempts to play the gracious loser.

Turning away with a grand and goofy, benign smile, Hedda marches right square into the arms of wild and wet Desi Arnaz. Guffaws break out from all corners, as Desi's bosom companions Hedda Gabler and John dos Passos anticipate a merry old contretemps. Ever the gentleman, Desi merely spits in Hedda Hopper's general direction. The other white Hedda and dos Passos rub their hands together in considerable glee (at least some of their hands); one slaps a knee. Meanwhile, irrepressible Dotty Parker is getting ready to goose absolutely everybody in sight, then start shooting (off her mouth). Hedda makes many malicious mental notes, on her way to stony perdition.

Observing in shadows from her cushy upper tier, Dorothy is grinning deeply, picturing how Desi would tell this story to laughing Lucy. Dorothy had long appreciated, and identified with Lucille Ball: a fellow, savvy Cold War cutie, who also crossed the color line with impunity—doubtless greatly sickening stalwart Hedda. Lucille Ball was investigated by HUAC in 1951. According to some critical historians, she donned her most famous persona—the scatterbrained "Lucy Ricardo"—in order to wriggle out of damaging allegations about her political sympathies. Ball was spared a recital of names by her obvious apoliticism and obsequiousness—she swore that she was never a member of the Party, but she had registered as a Communist voter in 1936 to please her Socialist grandfather. She also swore that she had not cast a vote for a Communist candidate.

7.
FIGHT THE POWER!

- In 1950, under Ronald Reagan's tenure as President of the Screen Actors Guild, the organization's Board of Directors drafted a loyalty oath. While the Guild professed to "fight against any secret blacklist," it stated that "if any actor...has so offended American public opinion that he has made himself unsaleable at the box office, the Guild cannot and would not want to force any employer to hire him." "In essence," Donald Bogle points out, "the Screen Actors guild condoned blacklisting."

  Among the black entertainers listed in *Red Channels* were Hazel Scott, Fredi Washington and Lena Horne (with whom the media was constantly comparing Dorothy, as if there was room for only one glamorous, black singer). Because of *Red Channels*, Horne later said that she was blacklisted from television appearances. At the time, Sidney Poitier was asked to sign a loyalty oath, just before he appeared in *Blackboard Jungle*. He refused, as he did when told to repudiate Paul Robeson and African American actor Canada Lee. The American public first learned of Poitier's refusals many years afterwards.

- In May '63, Dorothy joined Dick Gregory, Sammy Davis, Jr., Paul Newman, Joanne Woodward, and Rita Moreno at a rally for Martin Luther King, Jr. Over 50,000 people attended. "This is the largest and most enthusiastic civil rights rally in the history of this nation," King told the crowd that day.

  In July, Dorothy traveled to Chicago to attend the NAACP convention, and was a presenter at a Women's Auxiliary awards ceremony. She went on to Cleveland to be a guest co-host of the syndicated "Mike Douglas Show," where comedian Dick Gregory also appeared. In an interview with the city's African American newspaper, *The Call and Post*, Dorothy said: "Let's face it. It's the younger people who are opening up more avenues for the Negroes. It's their pressure and their unwillingness to be satisfied with the status quo that is causing the changes."

The taping of the Douglas show proved quite emotional as she talked to another guest, Dr. Gunnar Dwybad, executive director of the National Association for Mentally Retarded Children. In the glare of 50,000 watts of light, and with the unblinking eyes of video cameras, Dorothy looked straight ahead, and touchingly spoke of her daughter Lynn, the first and only time she did so on television. "It was one of the great moments in television drama," *Jet* commented. "Seldom, if ever has a star discussed a crushing personal problem with such frankness and intelligence." *Jet* also reported that Westinghouse was "so impressed by Miss Dandridge's sincerity" that they planned to show the videotapes on Boston, Baltimore, Pittsburgh and other outlets.

8.
BUT NONE OF THIS FILLED THE HUNGRY VOID

Languorous yet jazzy music is emanating from the snappy Cukaracha Club in ol' Mineola. Get ready for a mighty fine time. Caught dancing to the tin of a different drum was compelling CHARACTER X, with the well-known slit-eyes and puffy, puffy collagen cheeks. But guess which hot stud came mamboing by next?—and with nary a tummy tuck in sight!

Joey went off into a sidecar somewhere to brag about how much money he had made, yet at the same time was signing autographs for a buck on demented prescription pads, which had embossed on them, in big pink letters: "PRETTY PARTY-LINISH!" "I told him he was overexposed, and he needed to invest his money!" shrieked an agitated agent, at the peppy post-mortem. In any case, the $100,000 Stefano made in 1990 was due primarily to income from what may be called ancillary revenues: dancing at clubs and escort work, a more rarefied name for prostitution. Despite industry players' protestations that the days of exploitation in the business are over, the performers' video contracts are inherently exploitative.

In the mid '50s, Bettie enrolled in acting class at the renowned Herbert Berghof Studios of New York. Berghof was particularly pleased with her performance opposite fellow student Robert Culp in *The Dark Lady of Sonnets*, where she played a servant who had been caught making love to Queen Elizabeth's paramour, and would have her head cut off. When Berghof asked Bettie how she accomplished it, she told him that she had imagined how God would punish her for many sins. She acted in television shows such as the "U.S. Steel Hour," the "Eyewitness Show"; in summer stock, she was a hooker in *Camino Real* by Tennessee Williams, and had a small role in *Gentlemen Prefer Blondes*. When the Broadway auditions opened up for *L'il Abner*, Berghof urged Bettie to try out for the part of Moonbeam McSwine, but Bettie chickened out. "I didn't believe I could do it," she said in a 1995 *Playboy* magazine article. "I really lacked ambition in those days. I did nothing to promote myself."

Nevertheless, Bettie was highly sought after as a model, and had many decided public successes. Here at the Cukaracha Club, she sassily sambas like a semi-goddess. During most of the 1950s, it wasn't unusual to see Bettie's face smiling back at you on newsstands from Robert Harrison's tabloids, with captions like "Forbidden Sex Rites of the Tropics!" and "How We Licked the Teenage Sin Clubs." Harrison was an ex-newspaperman who had built a small empire of cheesecake magazines. His contacts in the entertainment business and his newspaper background forged important opportunities for Bettie. Harrison knew the press, and, more important, he knew how to get space in local columns.

With publicity in mind, Harrison took his new star model to the Beaux Arts Ball in 1951, at New York's Waldorf-Astoria. Bettie's high society debut was a "coming-out" in more ways than one—she appeared at the costume ball clad only in a pair of fishnet stockings, high heels, and twin telephone dials over her breasts. A box advertising the next month's cover of *Dare* magazine shielded Bettie's lower extremities. Bettie was a hit—her number got dialed more times that night than Grand Central Station's did in a week! At the close of the evening, she was crowned Queen of the Ball. Though the title was fleeting, it came with a full set of Revere cookware pots and pans.

Comfortably surveying the chatty Cuckaracha, Dorothy does not have to perform, nor are any of those too-vomit-making-for-words, right wing politicians likely to show up at this delicious out-of-the-way hot spot. Dorothy is here purely to check out the local talent, and to grudgingly admire the tacky, violet brocaded walls. Professionalism and years of experience carried her through chronic stage fright, to make a smash hit in the most chic Los Angeles and New York clubs. Her opening at

Manhattan's La Vie en Rose in January '52 was sensational. Phil Moore, at the piano, struck the chords. Then Dandridge, in a form-fitting gold lame gown, "came wiggling out of the wings," as *Time* later wrote, "like a caterpillar on a hot rock." Her voice was strong and, of course, sexy as she sang, "Love Isn't Born, It's Made." Her training and basic instincts as a dancer enabled her to move sensually and dramatically. Knowingly, she played with the song's suggestiveness. "Love isn't born on a beautiful April morn/Love isn't born, it's made/And that's why every window/Has a window shade." The house went crazy.

Patrons, including close friends Ava Gardner and Harry Belafonte, sat spellbound by her hot/cool style, her intelligent and sophisticated renditions. Throughout the performance, Dorothy was goddess-like, with a suggestion of fear. The day after the opening, *New York Post* columnist Earl Wilson called her "a singing sexation." But her friend Joyce Bryant said, "I don't think that Dorothy believed it. She was so terribly insecure. I heard it was the same thing night after night. She was just always frightened to death." The two-week engagement at La Vie En Rose stretched into 14 weeks, and led to tv appearances on Ed Sullivan's, Jackie Gleason's, and Steve Allen's shows, as well as major mainstream coverage in *Life*, *Look* and *Time*. Dorothy had long been a mainstay of *Jet* and *Ebony*, who sympathetically reported every rumor on all aspects of her intensely private life.

Dorothy, Bettie and Joey do a chillin' cha-cha, at the cookin' Cukaracha. They enjoy running into one another at Mogambo Bay Grille, or any reasonable facsimile: nod sympathetically, vaguely; belt down booze. On such an occasion, a sharp-eyed, in-the-know patron musingly mutters, "Fabulous yet fragile." "Or bitter?" replies another aching anchorite. Could that have been Himself? Ceaselessly scribbling, keenly bleary-eyed Peripatetic Book-Reviewer: patiently waiting (or so he'd have you believe) to assume center stage. Actually, that witty, would-be literary luminary could relate quite the lewd tale of recent wild experiments while ostensibly sedately waiting. But P B-R doesn't wish to wantonly whet your weary whistle, dear rapacious reader: suffice it to say this particular caper involved neither radio nor nun. Besides, he recently resolved (*after* wetting his own wanton whistle) that his ongoing role is to eschew egotism. Having enjoyed the uncomplicated comforts of remaining a technical/structuring device, P B-R imagines himself simply moving information around: afterwards, perhaps the Caribbean, or guillotine (if he's not so lucky).

Did ya know that one gorgeous night our glamorous trio nearly danced together? It happened like this: badly needing practice for an upcoming bar mitzvah gig, the unabashed Cukaracha band struck up a jazzy *hora*. Good and stoned, Joey immediately jumped up and began sliding and sinuously slinking: circling the rosy Rooster Room, flashing beguiling, come-hither looks. Bettie, exhausted from her day's photo shoot, was nonetheless inspired (not by Joey, as it turned out) to join another part of the human chain, carousing and gambolling, too.

Dorothy was not so inclined, having recently partaken in a memorable hoary *hora* at her friend Sammy Davis, Jr.'s gala birthday bash, held at Club Tirade in Bel Air's ultra chic Hotel de Dream. Between Joey and Bettie simultaneous thought-transmissions leapt across the flushed room: *if only I could establish eye contact, Dorothy would come dance with me, then make me famous*. Just as both seething sexpots were arranging uniquely ardent attempts at immortality—*accidentally coordinated*—Dorothy looked away to adjust her tattered dreams.

Alas, but for an averted glance.

9.
FACTS JUMP TRACK
Or, One Good Emission Deserves Another

Following the publicity of McCarthy's communist witchhunts, Senator Estes Kefauver—a Tennessee Democrat who was Adlai Stevenson's running mate for Vice-President in 1956—made a name for himself chairing a subcommittee on organized crime. Ironically, Richard Foster points out in *THE REAL BETTIE PAGE*, John Russell, the actor with whom Bettie shot her Twentieth Century Fox screen test, starred in a 1952 film loosely based on Kefauver's hearings. By 1954, he had turned his attentions to the evils of juvenile delinquency. His Senate subcommittee nearly shut down the comic industry, ending the careers of many Golden Age superheroes: bonfires were blazing in towns across the nation.

Kefauver unsuccessfully tried to link Bettie's bondage photos in *Cartoon and Model Parade* with the recent death of a seventeen-year-old Eagle Scout in Coral Gables, Florida. His body, trussed up like some of Irving Klaw's models, may have been engaged in autoerotic strangulation.

Klaw evaded arrest under a legal loophole for determining obscenity: such materials had to arouse or excite the "normal" person. The Feds finally ruled that Bettie's photos were appealing only to "certain types of sex perverts," partly because there were no men in them. Subpoenaed, Bettie waited for 16 hours in a witness room outside the chambers, but was never called in to testify. A popular tale holds that Bettie did appear before the subcommittee and, when asked by Kefauver what she thought of the bondage photos, she replied, "Why, Senator, honey, I think they're cute!"

Irving Klaw had hoped to avoid further trouble by moving his catalog business, but the local New Jersey police stormed the place, seizing inventory samples. The case was tied up in courts for another year-and-a-half, during which Congress instituted changes in the postal laws, making distribution more difficult. Eventually, facing a five-year prison sentence, Klaw offered to destroy his bondage and pinup negatives. Luckily, his sister Paula hid several sheaths of the negatives away, many of which were the photos of Bettie.

"Larry Flynt, he made no bones about what he was putting out, but there was no nudity at all in Klaw's stuff. He never showed a boob ever," Jack Bradley says passionately in defense of his former boss. In fact, Irving Klaw was so neurotic about avoiding nudity in his photos that he sometimes made his models wear two pairs of panties under their stockings, just to make sure no pubic hair showed.

After Bettie got out of cheesecake entirely, she drifted back to Florida and married Harry Lear, whom she met in Miami. Her behavior became increasingly bizarre: she was strict with Harry's children, and very orderly and methodical. Bettie would garden all night in the backyard, and developed strange ideas about Christianity: declaring that there was not one, but seven gods; she herself was their prophet. Leaving Harry, Bettie migrated to Bibletown Community Church in Boca Raton: this first of many Bible study experiences ended the night she was found running through the motel complex brandishing a 22-caliber pistol and shouting about God's retribution.

Harry brought Bettie home, precipitating the incident where she ordered the family, at knife-point, to stand in front of a picture of Jesus and pray: she was committed to Jackson State Memorial Hospital for four months, after Harry crawled out the bathroom window and phoned the police. Again returning home, Bettie soon lost control. According to police records, on that occasion she was put in a squad car, and later discovered there with dress pulled up, panties around her knees, and hands cuffed, masturbating with a coat hanger which had been left in the backseat. "Defendant psycho," the officer stated in the report, before driving her to the hospital to be treated for cuts from the hanger. (As you can well imagine, this is clearly the kind of tawdry detail which makes Foster's book so controversial—dubious and invasive—blinks P B-R, in the nod of an eye.) Charges of disorderly conduct and assault and battery were dismissed after Bettie voluntarily recommitted herself to Jackson Memorial's care: that stretch was six months, much of it spent under suicide watch.

10.
SHORT SHRIFT FOR DOROTHY?

You can imagine how reassuring that little pubic hair anecdote was to harried Hedda Hopper, who was *already* beside herself, planning her Easter get-up, in a round about sort of way. Hapless Hedda soon began to think almost constantly of pubic hair, and before you know it, her complexion cleared right up. (She remained an uptight, prejudiced fuck, though, with a "bully pulpit.") The Easter festivities turned out to consume the better part of a season—marjoram, rumor has it.

In this sagacious section, the Peripatetic Book-Reviewer makes a quizzical appearance (but he's not sure who's asking the questions); "Looking for coherence," is not his middle name. He *does* have a cogent analysis of similar qualities and societal functions of these 3 peculiar protagonists. However, Reviewer chooses not to share insights into author's intentions at this morning's gigantic gestalt/electroshock session: corporate heavyweights everywhere will simply have to cool hot heels.

Instead, Ancient Peripatetic uses this opportunity to question the writer's unhealthy preoccupation with Hedda Hopper—merely one of multitudinous, nauseating Hollywood right wingers, after all. Besides, unlike a rotting Ronald Reagan, Hedda was Woman Alone (see screenplay): briefly, fifth wife of much older Broadway actor, "Wolfie Hopper." Also somewhat unexplained is the writer's avid interest in the entrepreneurial career of Irving Klaw, whose photographs of Hollywood stars and pin-ups were first sold out of a struggling used bookshop, when Klaw also opened a mail order magic trick business.

Significant phases of Dorothy's career have been given short shrift in this cleverly abbreviated compendium, P B-R goes on to sharply observe, momentarily relinquishing coyness along with his own much heralded, single-mindedly technical approach. (Only you, dear reader, can imagine just how little certain friends disbelieved that particular pose.) Anyway, in commenting on the unfortunate omissions from Bogle's fine biography, Peripatetic Book-Reviewer graciously re-occupies his rightful position as wacky, moral mountebank.

During Dorothy's club successes, for instance, before *Carmen Jones*, she had yet to be offered a major film role, although several important movies about race were made: she had to watch white women being cast as light-skinned blacks—notably, Jeanne Crain in *Pinky*, and Ava Gardner in *Show Boat*. Later, after her Academy Award nomination for *Carmen Jones*, Dorothy was considered for many films including a remake of *The Blue Angel* (she particularly hoped to play Cherie in *Bus Stop*): nothing materialized for years.

Sidney Poitier, another prominent black actor of the period, was given parts which were "social symbols in an era that was beginning to have racial conflict—as well as civil rights—and more on its mind." But Bogle comments, "To ask Dorothy to play a social symbol in a film was like asking Elizabeth Taylor, Audrey Hepburn, Kim Novak, or Grace Kelly to perform as such. Cinema's glamorous and sensual goddesses had to play glamorous, sensual romantic roles."

Preminger insisted that Dorothy take only leading roles, and convinced her, against friends' advice, to reject the part of Tiptum in what became the hugely successful *The King and I*. Dorothy was always plagued by the idea of this as her fateful mistake, a turning point from which her decline dated. It did sour Twentieth Century Fox on Dorothy, where she broke a contact, which resulted in casting Rita Moreno, a lesser star. While Dorothy declared, "I can't play a slave," studio boss Darryl Zanuck believed he was giving her a break, as "an ethnic in fundamentally white movies."

Bogle believes that "Preminger, usually adroitly pragmatic and perceptive, was in this instance blind to movieland realities" of racism. Dorothy and Abby Mann often talked about the way Hollywood treated black women. "This is a terrifically racist town. I mean it was particularly then," said Mann. "I was shocked because in New York, it wasn't that way. But when I'd have black women at parties, it was new to California. It would almost be that they had to sleep around. Not even for parts or anything. But just to be part of the social milieu. In those days it was anticipated that no matter how attractive the girl was, if she was black, she was available. Dorothy was a big star. So they didn't see her that way. But I imagined what Dorothy had come through. She said she had to fight for her own turf and her own dignity."

Bogle vividly describes Dorothy's continuously growing isolation, and her sad end in September, 1965. Longtime friend Nat "King" Cole had died of cancer, at age 45. Cherished sister Vivian, who originally moved west with Dorothy and Harold Nicholas, couldn't parlay their childhood act into her own show business career. Vivian left town, and vanished entirely from Dorothy's, and their mother Ruby's, lives. As usual, Dorothy was only able to gain Ruby's attention in public situations, where she could bask in her daughter's fame.

Her friends were extremely wary of Dorothy's marrying sleazy Jack Denison, in whose wake ensued complete emotional and economic bankruptcy. Before their marriage, Denison pulled a gun on Dorothy. Once, after a quarrel, he stole personal photographs from her home, burned them, and mailed the charred fragments in a box with a note which read, "I will shoot you in your stomach. And you will be really sorry for what you are doing." At the end, many friends, old and new (especially the black actor Ivan Dixon) were available for Dorothy's "rambling, long and disturbing" late night phone calls; they could do little more than listen.

When Dorothy appeared at bankruptcy court, UPI photographers caught her in dark glasses. Humiliated, she only said that she had injured her eye in a fall; she couldn't stop crying. For Black America, it was a devastating image. Its dreamgirl, a splendid symbol of an independent, self-assured woman in *Carmen Jones*, was in the worst imaginable circumstances. No star's decline since that of Billie Holiday, asserts Bogle, had so affected the African American community.

11.
IN/VISIBLE DESIRE

The Mona Lisa? It was just a stupid painting!—Joey was more interested in checking out the curators.

Bettie was a VARGAS GIRL come to life. She pined for the sudsy stud of her past, the young diving instructor in Coral Gables; they had been so happy living together, and in periodic reunions.

A certain famous composer installed his special boys in a swank suite in the Beverly _____ Hotel. But Joey kept insisting, "I don't want a rich daddy to support me, I want to be independent." He surely followed his own yens when it came to making porn flicks: as soon as Joey yearned for some hot daddy to fuck him, coy Chi Chi crooked a convenient appendage.

Joey did have a genuine, caring, friend/patron who bailed him out all over the map, till the very end. Born in Buenos Aires, Dr. Alberto Shayo eventually gave up his medical practice to become an art deco dealer, and write a book about Deco sculpture, published by Abbeville Press. On the eve of his 26th birthday, Joey called Shayo from the Days Inn in New York to say goodbye: he had just slit his wrists, despondent that instead of paying off his debts, Joey had used the $3000 Shayo gave him to buy drugs. Joey expected Shayo to be more distressed about the money than his suicide attempt—a heartbreaking indication that years of selling sex had made Joey see all relationships as mercenary.

Shayo took Stefano home from the hospital for a few days. "He kept crying and told me how nobody had taken care of him. He felt he was washed up, his star status was fading."

Dorothy insisted, "I don't want a rich daddy, I want to be independent." Bettie repeated: "I don't want a rich daddy, I want to be independent." Producers, often with an adoring public, kept Joey, Bettie and Dorothy from insisting *too* much, by kindly administering a whopping dose of très trendy cultural anesthetic, or good ol' bonded booze; Bettie virtually imbibed God.

Joey was addicted to the moments of oblivion that only sex and drugs could supply. Small wonder. (Big dick!)

12.
CURTAIN CALLS

Alice is suitably seated at the base of the burgeoning mushroom. The crazy caterpillar smokes his hazy hookah, and the air is actually alive with psychedelic memorabilia. Clumsily, or cleverly, disguised as Peripatetic Book-Reviewer, the author himself diligently writes—*but he really needs to be weeping*. (We promise, faithful reader, this will be the solitary tediously suggestive outburst: we dearly wish we lived in a more robust age in which such obligatory, meta-textual interrogations and witticisms were altogether superfluous; alas.)

P B-R, looking disgruntled at best, immodestly declaims to an audience of enthusiastic nuts, in an olivey/walnuty amphitheater, somewhere underwater:

"This arcane monograph brilliantly illuminates the steep and icy dimensions of martyrdom that our trio, Icons of Utter Desirability, endured. Each one brought something totally unique into the permanent American erotic (and Dorothy, into the performative) imagination. For transgressing the original Puritan boundary, they suffered and died, as if on the cross. Each was destroyed by a personalized, lethal blend of familial abuse/neglect and vicious, unrelenting institutionalized oppression.

Further, these truly tragic divas embodied distinctive and imperative aspects of America's underground desires: longstanding, never before properly situated in an historical moment and figure. Their own stunning and unapologetic commercial existences stimulated the public into irreversible articulations of urgent desire.

Exotic Dorothy was the brocaded, elegant voluptuary; incredibly talented; sophisticated lady; a dish. Alluring Bettie had an outlandishly wholesome, outdoorsy verve for posing: 'the teasing girl-next-door, the eternal Queen of Curves.' Or, bound to sexy sisters, gaily gagging—'all business, sultry and serious, dominant and firm: Kitten with a Whip.' Doe-eyed and lewd exhibitionist Joey craved sex. Always in love with someone new, never having a steady boyfriend. Rather than positioning himself as object of others' desires, he proudly showed the whole, wide world how profoundly he could worship muscular studs; inside the mirror.

Sexually abused children; three lonely adults who needed to escape both into the public eye, and away from it. Expedient scapegoats, deeply baffled by interiority. Pioneer front-line warriors, in service of the eternal return of the repressed. Hyper self-conscious conceptual sculptors of America's libidinal fires."

Alice takes a hit off the hookah; the Queen of Tarts takes a back seat to love. So concerned is he about the harm done by glib over-generalization, not excluding his own, that Peripatetic B-R somehow forgets (how) to floss. However, the knave of custard (acting on behalf of her highness Ms. Tart) does tip his hat, grateful to Peripatetic One for finally spilling his guts regarding the purpose of all this dizzy dancing about.

The caterpillar's grin spreads even more widely (if less evenly) once the Playboy Channel is wired into his basic equipment. Meanwhile, ridiculous local news features a kooky Cheshire cat up a dusky, supposedly proverbial, tree. In China, absolutely everybody adores *The Titanic*; young and old alike hum its fulsome tunes.

A nickel for your dreams, baby.

Book 2
TWO MARGARETS

MARGARET FULLER: From
Transcendentalism to Revolution
Paula Blanchard
Addison-Wesley, 1987

EMERSON AMONG THE ECCENTRICS:
A Group Portrait
Carlos Baker
Viking, 1996

WOMAN OF VALOR: Margaret Sanger and
the Birth Control Movement in America
Ellen Chesler
Anchor Books, 1992

1.
THE BOOK AND THE LIFE

Paula Blanchard's excellent study of Margaret Fuller reveals a fascinating and complex character: America's foremost female intellectual and "woman of letters" of the 19th century (quite an oxymoronic notion then). Margaret was perceived as pedantic, plain (Oliver Wendell Holmes claimed she could resemble either a snake or swan, viewing her more as the former), competitive with men, and "unsexed": "a legendary bogeywoman, symbolizing a threat not only to the male ego but to the family, and thus to social order." The counter-coin-side was her reputation as a brilliant, witty and precise conversationalist—partly because, unlike many male counterparts, she actually responded to other speakers. Margaret's conversation, Emerson said simply, was the most entertaining in America. After a solitary childhood, she happily developed a talent for friendship, becoming a popular house guest and always maintaining a voluminous correspondence.

These skills led Margaret to earn her living from 1839-42 by teaching some of the most prominent and educated New England women, in subscription series of private seminars, or Conversations. The idea arose, and the nucleus formed for the first series, after Margaret became the natural center of the Transcendentalist group meeting informally at the bookstore Elizabeth Peabody had interrupted her teaching career to open, which offered for sale German and French publications that could not be found elsewhere in Boston. The regulars were often joined by two rather silent visitors, Nathanael Hawthorne and Horace Mann, the educational reformer recently instrumental in founding a State Board of Education, who were both courting Elizabeth's younger sister.

Whatever the topic of Margaret's individual discourses, she consistently strived for women to alter their self-image, by understanding that inadequacies were "a result of superficial education and the attitude of self-deprecation instilled by social custom." At the time, Fuller was the first editor of the Transcendentalists' influential review, *The Dial*, and its greatest contributor, along with Theodore Parker and Emerson, her most valued friend. She had already held several teaching positions of languages, including in a Providence school founded by a disciple of the abolitionist Bronson Alcott, whose own school was closed by the Boston authorities in 1840, when he admitted a black pupil. (Neither her teaching position at Alcott's Temple School nor the *Dial* ever ended up paying a cent; when Margaret resigned her editorship, Emerson declared "let there be rotation in martyrdom.")

The "peculiar intermixture" of Margaret's intellectual achievements and emotional evolution is particularly comparable to that of John Stuart Mill. Daughter of a former school teacher who was a Harvard graduate, Margaret's education was classical, rigorous and eclectic. By age 8, she had gone through Shakespeare, as well as Greek mythology, which brought on repeated, blood-drenched nightmares; at 9, Margaret was studying Virgil, Cicero, Livy and Tacitus. At 16, she was reading fluently in French, Italian, Latin and German: works by Petrarch, Dante, Milton, Racine, Epictetus, the romantic poets, Smollett. Margaret developed a lasting interest in Goethe, and began translating and writing about him. Praising contemporary, scandalous European women authors, Mme de Staël, George Sand and Mary Wollstonecraft, she went on to create a cornerstone of American feminist thinking, *Woman in the Nineteenth Century*, replete with classical paradigms and erudite literary allusions, underscoring her analysis of contemporary women's customary and legalized servitude in marriage. Drawing on the familiar Transcendentalist theme of self-reliance, Margaret advocated celibacy until a woman became strong enough to choose freely whether or not to marry.

Margaret's other major writings developed from changing locations and occupations. In the summer of 1843, she and a friend Sarah Clarke set out on a tour of what was still known as the American North-west—Chicago, Milwaukee, and surrounding countryside: her meticulous journal eventually became a book. *Summer on the Lakes* is a light but penetrating look into an ephemeral period in the history of the Great Lakes region, when the many diverse settlers, Norwegians, Germans, English, Irish, Welsh, remained in separate, homogeneous cultural oases. Margaret described the "generous, elemental landscape" in sharp contrast to the squalid ugliness and petty greed of the cities; she painted a disturbing picture of misplaced European city dweller settlers, and ruthless displacement of the Indians.

Margaret's reputation as a condescending and airy Transcendentalist notwithstanding, she worked very hard to help support her large family, and to assist the youngest of five brothers who was slightly mentally retarded to live independently as an adult, for one period at Brook Farm colony (Emerson also had a retarded younger brother, as did Walt Whitman).

In the country, at Groton, in 1832, she spent five to eight hours a day tutoring disinterested siblings, while helping in the "numbing routine" of enormous amounts of housework, particularly because her mother was often ill. She nursed her grandmother and two baby brothers, one of whom died in her arms. Later that year, her father died, too. As the eldest child, a thoroughly inexperienced Margaret had to disentangle his unfortunate financial affairs—the money was mostly tied up in unproductive real estate.

Later, Margaret moved to New York, and began a journalistic career. Horace Greeley, bohemian editor of the crusading *New York Tribune*, deeply admired *Woman in the Nineteenth Century* which was much talked about then; his wife had been an active participant in Margaret's Conversations in the Boston area. Greeley hired Margaret as literary editor: her reviews on theology, poetry, fiction, philosophy and history appeared on the front page. Greeley soon commissioned Margaret to do a series of articles on New York's philanthropic institutions. Fifth largest city in the world, New York boasted an admirable public transportation system, gaslights, a new water works, and an extensive network of institutions for the disadvantaged. Margaret visited Sing Sing prison and the

Bloomingdale Asylum for the Insane twice each, hospitals, orphanages, almshouses; she interviewed prostitutes in the Tombs, City jail. While depicting the Bloomingdale Asylum as a model of its kind, she refused to flatter New York civic pride, describing other establishments, along with local slums, in grimly dehumanizing terms.

Biographers tend to view Greeley as having saved Margaret from the "Never-Never-Land of Boston Transcendentalism," despite the fact that her companion on most of these visits was Boston Brahman William Channing, an ardent socialist and labor reformer. Margaret's last few years were lived in Europe, as correspondent for the *New York Tribune*, while simultaneous revolutions were erupting: she became well acquainted with Elizabeth Barrett Browning, Thomas Carlyle, George Sand, Chopin, the Polish patriot and leading epic poet, Adam Mickiewicz. Eyewitness to fervent revolutionary struggles, Margaret sent urgent and eloquent dispatches from besieged Rome during the 1848 uprising, where the Italian nationalist hero Giuseppe Mazzini was a very close friend; she was also writing a book about these events as they unfolded.

As independent thinker, Margaret was heir presumptive: both her grandfather and father had been rebellious intellectuals. The grandfather, Timothy Fuller, a minister without a congregation, was a respected delegate from Philadelphia to the Constitutional Convention in 1787: he refused to ratify the Constitution because it condoned slavery. Margaret's father, Timothy Jr., one of eleven children, was a debater at Harvard, elected to Phi Beta Kappa, and earned "something of a reputation as a gadfly," leading student protests against arbitrary college rules. There, young Fuller was a Unitarian among Congregationalists, a Jeffersonian Republican among Federalists, and an abolitionist among wealthy young men whose families owed much to slavery. His political beliefs cost him several potential lucrative jobs; later he was elected to the Massachusetts legislature, and four terms to Congress.

Just at the onset of her rigorous education, a sister Adelaide, two years younger, suddenly died, and Margaret was left to bear the full brunt of her father's keen pedagogical ambitions. But as she grew older, he began warning about "immoderate indulgence" in reading, and pushed

Margaret to learn the virtues of husband-procuring. She then developed symptoms which continued throughout her life: becoming melancholic, priggish, subject to violent tantrums. In conversation, she typically combined haughtiness with absolute candor. Emerson claimed that Margaret had no instinct for humility, and referred to her as "this imperious dame." The adult Margaret was frequently depressed, experiencing periods of lassitude and morbid religiosity, of which only her closest friends were aware.

Accepting the notion that it was impossible for her to be fulfilled both as a woman and a thinker, Margaret voluntarily denied her own interests in a number of younger men. She "assumed the mask of the brisk, self-reliant, neutered being," while dispensing "sisterly advice to her lovelorn friends." Compelled to periodically renew "vows of renunciation" in the face of the "quasi-erotic intensity of her friendships with both sexes," only in Europe did Margaret gloriously transcend that pattern: in Rome, she took a lover and had his child. Giovanni Ossoli was 26 when he met Margaret and spoke no English; he was tall and slightly built, good-looking, with a serious expression. The Ossolis were an ancient family of modest fortune which for generations had been in service of the papacy: his father had been an official at the Vatican before falling ill. Giovanni was "bred as a gentleman and indifferently educated, he was fit for no profession but the Army." There's no direct evidence that she and Ossoli ever married, but they remained a devoted couple. Reserved and self-sufficient, he respected, and was content to stay apart from, Margaret's intellectual work. A fierce Republican, Ossoli joined the civic guards, and was expecting to be killed when the French came in to put down the Roman triumvirate, led by Mazzini.

At age 38, Margaret went off to a village in the Abruzzi mountains, about 50 miles northeast of Rome, to have her baby. She explored the beautiful countryside alone, and continued to work on her book. But Margaret felt increasingly isolated, often unwell, the mail was censored, and she feared the Neapolitan soldiers who were swaggering about town: on their way to put down the liberals in Naples, they began warming up by arresting six there. She reluctantly left the baby, Angelo, with a wet nurse and returned to Rome, where revolutionary turmoil was rapidly accelerating. Margaret became director of one of the hospitals which her friend, the Princess Cristina Belgiojoso, started in abandoned ecclesiastical buildings (her own properties had been confiscated); after political exile, the princess organized her tenant farmers into a cooperative community, and built new housing, a school and a recreation center.

The couple finally decided on the necessity of leaving Italy, hoping to return in a few years. Exhausted, they made their way to England. Margaret went about preparing for a two-month sea voyage under a cloud of apprehension brought about by a prolonged headache. She saw evil omens everywhere. A steamer and sailing packet had recently been wrecked: both were reputedly safer than the merchant ship, *Elizabeth*, on which they were booked. They spent their last night in England with the Brownings, who teased Ossoli about a prophecy that he should fear death by water.

On the *Elizabeth*, their child became very sick, as he had once been in the mountains. Despite Margaret's characteristic fatalism, she again skillfully nursed Nino back to health. The *Elizabeth* came in sight of Fire Island, when it ran aground on a sand bar: the violence of the blow drove the cargo of marble through the ship's hull, flooding the hold. With the beach only a few hundred yards away, they awaited rescue. Although scavengers were visible on shore, there was never any sign of the rescue boat. Twelve hours later, a mountainous wave broke over the vessel, carrying away its mast and everybody who remained on board. Nino's body appeared on the beach a few minutes later; Margaret's and Ossoli's were never found. When news of the wreck reached Massachusetts, her brother-in-law Ellery Channing and Thoreau went to Fire Island for a week, to search for their bodies and personal effects.

2.
WHAT MAKES MARGARET RUN?

When Peripatetic Book-Reviewer sleepily read his email that hazy morning, he would have fallen right back asleep had he realized this would one day result in trading salty Fuller stories with crusty old coots at chic Cancun. In fact, P B-R believed he'd been asked to a symposium to help resuscitate Budd Schulberg's reputation, in which he (Aged One) played some small role long ago, having written his dissertation on social realism and the Hollywood dream machine. True, it was his policy to accept all free trips, but later P B-R realized that he had acted mostly out of nostalgia for an earlier phase of his own erstwhile career: when he still thought it possible to become a more or less established, if distinctly unspecialized, academic.

Budd Schulberg, you may recall, son of B.P. Schulberg, an original Hollywood mogul, was better known for his novels, *What Makes Sammy Run?* and *The Disenchanted* (about F. Scott Fitzgerald's last years) than screenplays. Schulberg, a left-liberal-anti-communist named 15 fellow Party members at the McCarthy hearings. Until he resigned in 1940, the Communist Party tried to shape his writings to become "useful weapons" as "proletarian novels." He's one of the few friendly witnesses that P B-R has found it in his none too capacious heart to forgive, chiefly because Schulberg cited the fate of the extraordinary Russian writer Isaac Babel as a primary reason for testifying. (A year later he wrote an article for *Saturday Review*, which discussed how the great Russian director Meyerhold was arrested and vanished, subsequent to a courageous public speech in 1939, also how Gorky died under mysterious circumstances, in 1936.)

Schulberg related that when he went, an avowed Young Communist, to the Writers Congress in 1934 in the Soviet Union, Isaac Babel spoke publicly for the first time since 1928: he was clinging to the right to write badly, which Schulberg didn't understand then. Eventually, every one of the speakers at that Congress was liquidated. Further, when Schulberg confronted Lillian Hellman about Babel's fate—he had fought in the Russian Revolution, only to be killed later in a Stalinist death camp—she responded, "Prove it!" Schulberg went on to write the screenplays for *A Face in the Crowd* and *On the Waterfront* (which exonerates "snitching" and was directed by Elia Kazan, another notorious friendly witness). Continuing to write, in 1964 Schulberg helped found the Watts Writers Workshop where he remained active.

Not until re-reading his email several days later did Book-Reviewer realize the conference didn't concern Schulberg at all; luckily, that message was still in his trash, along with the computer dating service's demand to pay the bill and immediately cease his heartless lying. Too late! P B-R had already wired his agreement to appear (shut)—not to mention pre-spending the meager honorarium toward a shiny new root canal. Although he didn't know exactly who had invited him to this "WHAT MADE MARGARET RUN?" symposium, P B-R presumed it was due to his recent research on female abolitionists in relation to the Transcendentalists: his article had focussed on the violent, large scale uprisings against returning the slave Anthony Burns, who was hunted down in Boston in 1854. At the Framingham Independence Day celebrations, Quaker activist Abby Kelley Foster, Sojourner Truth, Thoreau, William Lloyd Garrison and others argued for massive disobedience to the Fugitive Slave Law.

So, in true, erratic scholarly fashion, P B-R began to read and ponder Margaret Fuller's fascinating life and career, whereas previously she'd been an occasional side dish to Thoreau's tender thorns. Soon P B-R believed that he could whip out a pertinent little paper. He knew Fuller had become a full-blown abolitionist only after she left the country, and witnessed the European revolutions: formerly, she and her father had both advocated the gradual phasing-out of slavery, much to the distress of her close friend, Lydia Maria Child, editor of the *National Anti-Slavery Standard*.

The more P B-R pondered, the more ponderous he became, until he felt like he resembled a bloated Emerson. Scarcely anyone could comprehend this man in the supermarket, or abroad. Nevertheless, he stood as he would. Typically, at the conference itself, P B-R managed to emit cogent remarks, sometimes posing as Mrs. Margaret Mytholee of Ithaca, or else Oliver de Prongh, self-styled "universal live-wire, ex Eye-Ball, etc.": mainly de Prongh materialized to cruise ladies of both sexes at Cancun Hilton's decidedly cocky Cukaracha club.

Overhearing vague talk that a subsequent conference might occur in idyllic Vancouver, on the plane home P B-R quickly began jotting down a list for future thought, and possible articles (hopefully not for academic journals): "WHAT IS TO BE LEARNED?" Number one: the high infant and childhood mortality rate. How could Margaret's generation stand that awful fact of life? Another major issue concerned how similar Margaret's familial patterns were to other exceptional women's (and not just from her own generation)—feminists, abolitionists, Socialists, labor organizers. For instance, to Margaret Sanger and Simone de Beauvoir: all had domesticated and supportive mothers along with strongly intellectual, individualist fathers whose financial losses exposed unanticipated inadequacies; adoring daughters precariously thrust into position to cope with harsh exigencies. Although most biographers believe that Margaret's own pious mother exerted little influence, Blanchard sees Margaret Crane Fuller as imparting many domestic skills, and the love of her garden, to her daughter.

One definite psychographic area for someone to bubble around in is Margaret's significant attachments to a number of older women (not to mention younger men!): beginning at age 7 when she developed a strong devotion to Ellen Kilshaw, a visitor from Liverpool; Margaret's parents were hoping Ellen would remain to become her teacher. A model of British good taste and poise, Ellen played the harp and painted in oils. At age 25, Margaret was fortunate to become the protégée of Mrs. Eliza Rotch Farrar, a handsome woman in her forties, second wife of John

Farrar, professor of mathematics and natural philosophy at Harvard who introduced Margaret to Cambridge society, offering her a second home. The maternal Eliza Farrar helped to transform Margaret into a poised and graceful young lady, supervising her hairdresser and seamstress; within a few years, Margaret had earned a reputation for irreproachable taste in clothes. She finally met Emerson in 1836 at the Farrars' soiree for Harriet Martineau, the English Unitarian and writer of semifictional books on social reform. Eliza Farrar's autobiography, published at age 75, revealed a history of transAtlantic connections: as a young girl she had known Lord Nelson and Lady Hamilton, Maria Edgeworth, Mrs. Siddons the actress, and had once been at a salon of the famous beauty, Madame Recamier (whose ardent relationship with Madame de Staël Margaret wrote about, and wished to emulate in similar relationships with women).

Peripatetic Book-Reviewer barely got a chance to expand his original list of topics, let alone do any pondering, before summer was a fluky memory—actually, the month long trip to the east coast didn't leave much time or money. Now that the new semester was unrelentingly puffing away, Peripatetic One felt like he might as well be teaching ancient Finnish epics to over-age, pre-operative pundits. Plus, he had foolishly dreamed of designating whole juicy research areas to particular juicy grad students. If only he hadn't abdicated his cushy tenured position in cultural anthropology at Harvard to take that perilous plunge into tin stars in a small mining college in suburban Colorado (mumbling something about an LSD experience in which he truly grasped the meaning of "academic freedom"), he could still have grad students galore to mop up the blood, dutifully worshipping every desultory drip.

3.
A LITERARY LI(F)E

Back in San Diego ("oy, homebase") to teach his standard "new journalism" courses, P B-R was ruminating that although he'd eagerly left a too provincial feeling Colorado only a few weeks before, it already seemed like a lifetime—at least he wasn't run out of town, like in unspeakable Duluth. (How *had* that spotted cow gotten into his studio, anyhow?) Upon returning, P B-R promptly learnt that Anne was dying of cancer; she'd been sick the past year, without anybody at school appearing to know much about it. Close friends many years ago, still with a strong affinity, P B-R called several times; they gossiped and laughed, but when he said he wanted to visit, Anne replied, "Please don't"—no possibility of laughter there.

P B-R had many intimates who had died of AIDS or cancer, of course, but none in the past two years. Trying not to dwell on any of this (despite those individuals being on his mind almost daily), P B-R began casting around for a diverting and manageable writing project: he got an idea when some friends, who came over to play cards and *Clue*, jokingly started casting the *Margaret Fuller Story*. The big budget version would star either Jodie Foster or Lili Taylor—Taylor might also be induced to appear in the independent feature. Jonny Depp would obviously be ideal for Count Ossoli; understandably, one faction insisted on Gary Oldman. Opinion was also divided as to whether Lyle Lovett would make a more convincing Thoreau or Emerson. For the young Emerson, there was a comic yet oddly heated debate on the virtues of Joaquim Phoenix vs. a cravat clad Winona Ryder. For the made-for-tv-movie, they couldn't think of any youthful equivalents of staples such as Lindsay

Wagner, Meredith Baxter Birney or Tom Skerrit (a plausible father in all 3 versions, they concurred).

The story would open in England, on the night before Margaret and Ossoli's fateful sailing, with gracious Elizabeth Barrett Browning (Patti Smith?) hosting a gala farewell party: establishing the couple's significance while affording juicy cameos, like Heather Locklear (or Patty Hearst) as George Sand. They debated having Keats and the Shelleys present, mostly to weave a Frankenstein subplot into the film—Cristina Ricci would make a wonderful Mary Shelley, and James Brolin a divine Frankenstein!—figuring nobody would recognize or care about a small anachronism. But in case any critics were unable to assent to this patently pomo aesthetic, they had fictionalized a certain Kelley and Sheats, possibly to be played by identical twins; John thought both might be powerfully portrayed by Courtney Love.

The very next morning, P B-R began composing this telling tale:

I passed the summer of 1816 in the environs of Geneva. The season was cold and rainy, and in the evenings we crowded around a blazing wood fire, which cackled like a howling ode. Occasionally we amused ourselves with some German stories of ghosts, which happened to fall into our hands. These tales excited in us a playful desire for imitation. Two other friends (a tale from the pen of one of whom would be far more acceptable to the public than any thing I can ever hope to produce) and myself agreed to write a story, founded on some supernatural occurrence.

The weather, however, grew serene; and my two friends left me to take a journey among the Alps, and lost, in the magnificent scenes which they later present, were all their ghostly visions. The following tale is the only one completed:

I awoke one morning, and began my usual ablutions, when I was quickly overcome by an attack not of dizziness exactly, rather eeriness. My familiar pink tiled bathroom felt alien, slightly malevolent. I couldn't remember if I was at home or somewhere on the road, in the midst of travels. Then, I saw her standing there, the ghost of my recently deceased soul-mate, Kathy Acker: vibrant, sunny, knowing, brilliant, looking like no ghost of which I could conceive.

Kathy beckoned me to follow. Without even brushing my teeth, I left the house, or passed through its pulsating portals. Outside, we were on a concrete patio which had many broken old tv sets scattered around its perimeters, weeds growing haphazardly in the cracks. With a wave of relief, I realized that we were in the pleasantly run-down seaside shack where I had resided in my student years; Kathy was also a graduate student, living nearby with her younger, composer lover and several cats. The blue blue sky was broad and dotted with glorious, puffy white clouds, which seemed dense but like they might precipitously vanish. Down the hill, the shining sea called. We were so happy to be alive, and together.

The noise of Spanish dance music trumpeted seductively. Peering behind the house, where formerly a small vegetable and marijuana garden had provided us with mucho nourishment, I found a makeshift wooden structure—imagining it a captivating cabana in a small Mexican seaside resort. I thought about the Sea of Cortex, for some reason. We noticed that drinks and sandwiches were being served, so we entered the haunted refreshment area.

A number of disconsolate individuals sat stiffly at separate tables; a few obvious expatriates, and quasi-Eurotrash tourists, were reading thin volumes of rhymed verse. Kathy raised a dubious eyebrow, murmuring that the tattered appearance of this place should really have drawn a more buoyant and funky crowd. We were getting ready to make our way down to the beach, when a distraught yet lithe man rushed into the enclosure, breathing heavily, "*le migra*," trying to blend into the woodwork.

Suddenly, several inert patrons unexpectedly sprung into action. Motioning for the recent bearded arrival to join them, one sedate Englishwoman handed him old-fashioned writing implements and a spanking new Baedecker's. They hurriedly dressed the refugee in an inexpensive fedora, and cheap but trendy paisley, suggesting that if the police arrive, he speak only Russian. Surprisingly, he responded fluently in what sounded like the mother tongue all right, shyly smiling his thanks. People at other tables nodded their approval; some began to spoon.

Kathy and I sat back down at a table speckled in sunlight, and ordered cassis, though I didn't quite know what that meant. We grumbled about how awful grad school was, despite our studying dyspeptic and witty old Jonathan Swift. Then we laughed again about the grotesque reading we had recently attended in New York, in which the bourgeois essayist Philip L. ____ prattled on about his newly renovated loft in Soho, and a très naughty dog who simply *refused* to stop peeing on the darling wooden floors.

The *migra* never appeared. As the afternoon shadows lengthened, more and more immigrants wandered in, their tattered rucksacks bearing precious photographs: perhaps a cameo or old-fashioned piece of jewelry, maybe a bit of provolone or passion fish. Weary and suspicious, nonetheless most seemed immensely relieved to have arrived at this charming canteen. Ostentatiously sighing, they took seats, ordered ceviche and Dos Equis. The music and chatting grew louder yet more languorous.

These sweet and shell-shocked souls became almost merry. Oddly, a number of them somehow knew Esperanto; many also spoke Spanish and some English. Photos of loved ones accompanied funny, fortunately not-too-lengthy anecdotes told around the heartily decorous outdoor fireplace. Dancing commenced. Our original refugee was now back in faded cut-offs and sandals, standing by the fence, staring wistfully out to sea. He began to jump up and down to the captivating samba music.

At first, flailing in futile escape gestures, he could only move in place, frantically kicking his heels higher and higher. After awhile, partly because nobody visibly reacted, this lovely man's motions became increasingly rhythmic, his expression concentrated and joyful, *released*. His droopy eyes were simultaneously more lucid and narcotic; sometimes, he reminded me of himself! His laugh was that of a beaming boy turning green. Kathy and I suddenly knew that we were sharing a wonderfully improbable moment: there in this sprawling seaside cabana in a town so plainly doomed to horrific gentrification, solace in communion was temporarily granted us all.

Weeks later, my dear comrades returned from their mountain trek, and I read them my tale. When the name "Kathy Acker" was first uttered, Kelley and Sheats started, as if harkening to a distant star; shortly, both poets were weeping. Sheats sadly opined: death comes far too early to genuine artists, the very people vitally needed to grow old, and truly be identified as the public's seers and healers. Instantly, we all had a foreboding of never reaching the age at which it would become necessary to practice steely indifference. A collective shiver was followed by lissome Sheats quickly adding, not without a soupçon of slyness, "Still, we are already immortal—*and we know it.*"

So we rushed down to the sea, to feel a tiny toehold on eternity. The rain had stopped: egrets were cutting capers in the moonlight; sudsy surf shimmering. Lucid and lovely. But Kelley (and perhaps Sheats) abruptly caught sight of the doomed ship *Elizabeth*, tilted upright in the sand bar; anguished Margaret Fuller clutching her baby, seemed to sight them too—distant onlookers, safely ashore. I also had a momentary, stark glimpse of the ghostly *Elizabeth*, pounded by waves of death. Instinctively, I tried to forget, and stay grounded: pondering the preparation of pungent leek soup, for the coming midnight repast. Little did I realize how impossible that simple task would soon prove to be.

4.
THE ETERNAL TRIANGLE
Or, Love Is Square

Margaret Fuller witnessed the marriage of the two people she was most in love with: Anna Barker and Sam Ward. It was Margaret's fervent conviction that they were both all which she herself was not: gracious, handsome, wealthy, plus possessing none of her ungainly, and implacable ambitions. Anna Barker was a fresh, exquisitely captivating spirit. Upon first meeting her, Emerson wrote, "She had not talents or affections or accomplishments or single features of conspicuous beauty, but was a unit and whole, so that whatsoever she did became her...She had an instinctive elegance...No princess could surpass her clear and erect demeanor...Her conversation is the frankest I ever heard. She can afford to be sincere. The wind is not purer than she is." Whenever Margaret was inclined toward playing Madame de Staël, Anna was forever her rapturous Madame Recamier.

Seven years younger (in other words, exactly the right age for her), Sam Ward was a passionate devotee of fine arts, about which Margaret knew very little until the pair literally pored over thousands of prints and sketches that Sam had brought back from his two-year grand tour of Europe: a reward for graduating from Harvard College, of which, in addition to the Boston Athaneum, his father was treasurer. Margaret first met Sam the year before, on a party which journeyed by steamboat to the upper Hudson with its spectacularly scenic gorges and deep ravines. Some twelve miles north of Utica, Margaret and Sam took a long walk at Trenton Falls, where they came upon a clump of snowdrops at the foot of a rock. "It passed quick," Margaret wrote to Emerson, "as such beautiful moments do, and we never had such another."

That union of two adored ones, Sam and Anna, was engineered by the same surrogate mother who initiated Margaret into the elite, intellectual circles she so craved, who arrranged the steamboat journey where she met Sam, and who later introduced him to Anna. Eliza Farrar and her husband accompanied Sam on his European tour, where Eliza's cousin Anna joined them. More than anything, Margaret had wished to go to Europe. She was planning on it, until her father's death threw his family into a state of genteel poverty. Instead, she went to work, while the beloved rich and beautiful ones traveled in style, falling in love under Eliza's glowing sanctions.

Soon after returning, Sam announced his engagement. But Anna broke it off until Sam agreed to give up a potential career in fine arts to go into his father's bank—hopefully, Margaret derived some satisfaction from that ultimatum. Sam and Anna's liaison prompted many "vows of renunciation": a chief component of Margaret's "quasi-erotic intensity of friendships with both sexes." The belief that she was "not yet purified" led Margaret to think of Vestal Virgins, and she wrote, "Let the lonely Vestal watch the fire till it draws itself and consumes this mortal part."

The message Margaret mirrored from all quarters was ancient, deeply familiar: don't even consider trying to be both a woman of letters and a woman. You are unsexed. *Sacrifice desire*. This life of the flesh is not yours; *it is our life*. As the American oratario drew to a close, Margaret ripped off her own pantaloons, positively insisting that someone else dutifully wipe up the tear-stained chiffonier. *Blood of our blood, we rise again to live.*

5.
ENTER MARGARET SANGER, RIDING PLUMED DESIRE

Margaret Louisa Higgins, born in 1879, was fortunate to come of age in the next century's exuberantly bohemian spirit of Greenwich Village's heyday: no morbid Vestal renunciations for her! Triumphantly, she managed to have it all, including many lovers largely simultaneous with two marriages. In Margaret Sanger's uniquely brilliant, 50-year career, she developed a network of independent birth control clinics and engineered a major movement: transforming women's rights and access to birth control services worldwide.

Margaret's most famous lovers were H.G. Wells and sexologist Havelock Ellis, who suffered premature ejaculation: that didn't rule him out—"then about 65% of American men could be called sexually impotent," she wrote. Margaret began several other liaisons in England while in the process of ending her first marriage to William Sanger. A number of these affairs continued for decades after she married her second husband, Noah Slee, a multimillionaire manufacturer who was 61 when he met 42-year-old Margaret. Beguiled, Noah pursued Margaret tirelessly, with the "ardor of an adolescent." He stood by her side during the infamous arrest at Town Hall in 1921, and for almost a year on a round-the-world lecture tour.

Margaret described Noah "as a babe in the woods—a deprived and hungry man with the passions of a youngster." It is unclear to Margaret's biographer, Ellen Chesler, if Noah knew about his wife's lovers, most of whom he met on the couple's trips to England. She would often write torrid letters to them while in bed with Noah (such as desiring kisses in "precisely two places"). Once, writing to him from London, she made this slip (which she corrected), "Dearest Noah—Darling—It is really always lovely to be away from you even for one day." She meant *lonely*. Frequently traveling abroad without him, Margaret organized international conferences and established new clinics; on several highly publicized trips to India and Japan, she had invigorating meetings with Gandhi, Nehru and other world leaders.

Noah had been married for more than 30 years to Mary Roosevelt West, with whom he had two sons and a daughter. (He described his wife as so cold that each child cost him dearly in gifts of diamonds and pearls.) A manufacturer of his own 3-in-One Oil formula, Noah was a pillar of the establishment, active in the socially impeccable Union League Club and Episcopal Church affairs in New York City, where he administered a Sunday school: whenever Margaret told the story in later years, she swore that she had nearly fainted when she first heard of this.

Noah built a stately home for them several hours north of New York City; they also had separate apartments in the same building in lower Manhattan (he didn't have her key). Noah helped Margaret's birth control organizations to run on a more professional basis, and became their primary private benefactor. He had large quantities of rubber-spring diaphragms shipped from Holland and Germany to his factory in Montreal, then smuggled them into New York in 3-in-one Oil containers. When the clinic ran into a problem securing the necessary spermicidal jelly Noah manufactured the German formula clandestinely at his New Jersey plants.

Margaret had previously married William Sanger, a young Jewish architect and stained-glass artisan, in 1902, after less than six months of furious courtship; the couple moved to Manhattan in 1910. Then, the era was described by the writer Floyd Dell as a "glorious intellectual playtime"—a period of optimism before wars, fascism and repression created the sober and enduringly grim realities of the century. In 1911, the Sangers joined the active New York chapter of the Socialist Party of America. Margaret was soon writing about birth control for the Party's nationally distributed daily, *The Call*. William put his professional skills to use by documenting the building code violations which had led to the tragic decimation of the Triangle Shirtwaist Factory fire.

The Sangers were an integral part of Mabel Dodge's salons, where bohemian artists volatilely mixed with activists, such as Emma Goldman and Alexander Berkman, the Harvard educated John Reed, and Wobbly organizers Elizabeth Gurley Flynn, and "Big Bill" Haywood. Margaret lectured on sexuality and family limitation at the Ferrer Center, also known as the Modern Center, founded in 1910 by anarchists and radicals to commemorate Francisco Ferrer, the free-thinker who had set up a network of schools in the Spanish countryside to educate the masses for participatory, democratic rule: Ferrer's execution at the hands of monarchists in a Barcelona prison a year earlier had provoked an international outcry.

With its roots in political, economic and anticlerical insurgency, the International Modern School Movement quickly developed into more than an educational experiment in keeping with such contemporary innovators as Montessori, Piaget, and Dewey. In New York, the Ferrer Center established itself as a forum for labor and cultural radicalism; Clarence Darrow, Lincoln Steffens, and Alfred Stieglitz were associated with it. In addition to the children's program, the school featured evening classes in socialist theory with Goldman and Berkman, Jack London, and Upton Sinclair; the realist painter George Bellows and the young modernist Man Ray gave art lessons, Eugene O'Neill and Theodore Dreiser taught writing.

The spirit of the Village was reflected in two significant cultural events: one was the 1913 Armory exhibition, which showcased Cubism, Post-Impressionism and abstract painting. For the first time, New Yorkers were introduced to a dazzling array of modernist European art, including works by Renoir, Gaughin, Cezanne, van Gogh, Redon, Matisse, Vlaminick, Picasso, Kandinsky, Duchamp, Picabia, Delaunay and Dufy. Preceding the Armory show by several months was the impressive Pageant in the old Madison Square Garden in which 1200 striking silk workers from Patterson, New Jersey vividly dramatized their plight to 15,000 spectators.

A group at Mabel Dodge's concocted the Pageant; Margaret worked intensively with John Reed to stage it. Crowding onto ferries from Hoboken to Manhattan, strikers then marched up Fifth Avenue singing the "Marseillaise" and the "Internationale." With an immense IWW sign, and a flaming red stage as their backdrop, they recreated their walkout and picketing of the mills, the relocation of their children, the arrest of protestors, and the death of a bystander (whose family was seated in a box in the audience). Spectators joined them and Wobbly leaders in revolutionary chants and songs, as a coffin was carried down the aisles to the stage, and many strikers individually placed red carnations on the casket.

Margaret always remained faithful to the free love ideal, Chesler notes, even "long after others of the Village crowd had retreated in confusion and unhappiness to a monogamy that became acceptable simply with maturity or...as the result of intensive psychoanalysis." But she was no dewy-eyed idealist. At that point in her life, she already had three children under the age of 10 to support. One of a poor family of 11 children, Margaret trained early as a visiting nurse and midwife. Working part-time with Lillian Wald's Visiting Nurses Association in the immigrant districts of the Lower East Side, Margaret found "only degradation and despair," according to Chesler, "unlike Wald and the legions of economically secure men and women who swelled the ranks of the social settlement houses" for whom working with the poor was a socially rewarding experience.

Margaret blamed both parents for their ignorance of birth control, otherwise admiring her free-thinking father; she was unable to acknowledge her mother's deeply felt religious convictions, particularly in several later autobiographies. While never openly defying her husband by baptizing the children or attending mass, Anne remained a pious Catholic, praying in private, and receiving baskets of food for her family from the parish priest. In fact, contraception information, though flawed, was widely circulated during Margaret's childhood. Until the obscenity statutes of the 1870s, contraception was advertised in almanacs and mail order catalogues; thereafter, a covert trade prospered.

In England and the U.S., mass distributed pamphlets advocated the use of sponges and other occlusives, postcoital douching, as well as coitus interruptus. "Fountain syringes," or douche bags were staples of mail-order houses, along with many different "sanitive" powders or suppositories, from the relatively harmless bicarbonate of soda to potential toxins such as carbolic acid. (In the 1920s, the best selling douche was Lysol, the household cleaning agent.) Young women whose marriages were announced in local newspapers received circulars in the mail, for products sold under the ubiquitous euphemism of "feminine hygiene" in respectable farm journals and women's magazines.

Margaret's notoriety as a birth control advocate thrust her into the national leadership of the movement from 1915 on, when she fled the country (which also facilitated her final break up with William Sanger) to avoid prosecution under the heinous Comstock laws: Margaret was charged with 4 criminal counts, carrying a maximum sentence of 45 years, for disseminating information about sexuality and contraception through the mails. Temporarily leaving her children, she traveled throughout the British isles, lecturing and participating in organizing local birth control advocacy groups.

That summer, Margaret was often in the company of Havelock Ellis. Although they would never again be lovers, as with H.G. Wells, the friendship was lifelong; in later years, Noah subsidized Ellis. He introduced Margaret to his circle, and she became intimate with Ellis' new lover, Françoise Cyon. Margaret began several passionate new, longterm affairs there, including with Hugh de Selincourt, a handsome patrician and novelist. (Soon, Havelock Ellis despised Hugh who went on to have an affair with Françoise Cyon.) Margaret and Hugh's relationship was "unabashedly physical"; her letters to him are described as "gushy and graphically sexual."

Selincourt brought Margaret to Wantley, the countryside estate where his aristocratic wife Janet lived, with whom he was no longer having a sexual relationship, and their talented pianist daughter, Bridgette. (Later, Noah became known as "the squire" there; Hugh was called "the poet" and Havelock Ellis was referred to as "the King.") This arcadian retreat was a 16th century stone house which had once belonged to Percy Shelley's father. The liberated de Selincourts were committed to recreating the "morally unconstrained universe that Shelley and his soulmate Lord Byron had pursued in exile from Italy some 100 years earlier."

Harold Child, a well-known editorial writer and critic at the *Times* in London, shared the house: he was Janet's lover prior to his involvement with Margaret. Chesler reports that "the various and complicated couplings of the Wantley circle were apparently never concealed from the larger group." In 1924, in a letter to her friend Juliet Rublee (the feminist philanthropist who played a key role in mobilizing support from wealthy women on the east coast), Margaret confided that she had spent the night with Hugh, and that Harold and Janet were also on hand to celebrate her return; she and Janet had "an embrace beyond any earthly experience."

6.
MORE FUNERAL SERVICES

One fine Spring morning, P B-R found himself lazing around with Steve in a big old Victorian house in Berkeley (where they'd never actually been together), happily talking at their leisure. While this featured none of the crisp photo realism of those dead friend dreams which P B-R sometimes fancied were visitations, he *was* able to linger, using a lucid dreaming technique he'd recently researched for a popular science writer. Awakening, P B-R instantly felt an acute longing for Steve, his first close friend who'd died of AIDS; then he remembered that today was Anne's funeral services.

John and Rae picked up P B-R. The 3 old friends were considerably better dressed than their usual teaching garb—not wearing black highlighted the solemnity of the occasion. As Anne's admiring but distant colleagues, both Rae and John were quietly solicitous of P B-R's state of mind. Driving to the Congregational church a few blocks from Anne's home—an upper-middle class black neighborhood, east (of course) on the freeway, on a mesa above the "ghetto," with spectacular views of Tijuana many miles to the south—they listened to the stunning used CD that John had found. Anne reading her lucid poems to a jazz accompaniment: her mellifluous voice a canny instrument.

The mourners were gathering into 2 groups: family and congregation, all black, milling around the parking lot, women at the core; the UCSD literature faculty and staff, hispanic and white, who had mostly known Anne best in her early, active years there. P B-R embraced several of them, standing in a tight cluster around the church entrance. Carlos appeared. Staring wordlessly into each other's eyes, they kissed on the cheek, his expression wide-eyed, frozen grief; turning away, P B-R burst into sobs. Not that they were friends—P B-R hadn't seen Carlos since he retired. But both had been intimate with Anne early on in the '70s, at this new and ostensibly progressive campus, in this old and definitely reactionary city: P B-R, the activist and perpetually reluctant grad student; Anne, a young faculty member, the first black and one of the first tenure-track women in the department; Carlos, its most radical founding member. Later, they all bitterly witnessed the window of opportunity and hope come crashing in for minorities: plummeting of California's economy and schools, decimation of affirmative action, prisons sprouting like fierce mushroom clouds.

Inside the spacious and airy, modern church, they immediately encountered 2 heartbreaking, blown-up photos of a young, luminous Anne: P B-R was *really* thankful the casket was closed, and only the family would go on to the cemetery. With sudden conviction, he felt a rush of gratitude that Anne had told him not to come visit: she'd deliberately spared him. When the gospel choir ended, and the first eulogy began, concerning Anne coming up from stark poverty to major intellectual achievements as a poet and scholar, P B-R's limbs started to tremble; Rae leaned over and just kept her hand on his arm. He found her physical proximity immensely reassuring.

Each speaker was thoroughly eloquent. A young woman stepped forward from the chorus to state how comforting Anne had been when her own son was killed. Her niece talked about Anne's sending her through an elite, La Jolla private school, the only black in the class, then crucially assisting in struggles to graduate from UCLA as a single mother. Crying, she said her family was a small set of women whom Anne had inspired to be fierce fighters. Anne's parents, and 2 of her 3 sisters had died young, mostly from cancer, too—her parents had been farmworkers (the family exposed to God only knows what chemicals). Anne's brother-in-law from Phoenix described her as a strong personal ally, and staunchest supporter of family members' educations. Two former female colleagues, one now an administrator at UC Santa Cruz, the other a professor at

Emory, related charming and pointed anecdotes of Anne's tenacity as a new faculty member, advocating for widespread minority inclusion.

P B-R felt particularly shaky when Becky's fragile mother got up to speak: Anne had always been part of that sadly diminishing family; she and Becky had been inseparable, like sisters. Tragically, Becky had died in her early 40's: her heart giving out from too many diet pills and losing too much weight too quickly. Anne clearly never recovered from the loss of her constant companion. P B-R used to love hanging out with them, smoking pot, and constantly laughing; he thought they were about the funniest people, and sharpest observers, he'd ever known, as they riotously "read" everyone's various pretensions. (P B-R and Becky had occasionally done coke together, but that quickly stopped when he realized her coke problem was at least as bad as his own.)

The minister emeritus delivered the most powerful, and the most political, eulogy P B-R had ever heard at any memorial, in or out of church. An elegant, grey-haired, light-skinned man with a cane slowly ascended to the pulpit: "When Anne Johnson learned that the Regents had rescinded affirmative action at the University of California, she was sorely grieved," he began in thunderous tones. The gravely disappointed congregation members had charted a bus to tour several of the Southern black colleges which their denomination originally founded. At an important meeting upon their return, Anne admonished them to stay proactive, focussed on the future, and not on past achievements; they must continue to view themselves as agents of change, rather than objects of others' charity or generosity. Their debt to Anne was profound: she appeared as an invaluable, fundamental link to the university and intellectual communities—*dead at age 53.*

The eulogy was astonishing for capturing Anne's spirit so vividly: unwavering commitment to education (which included writing an award winning children's book about picking cotton), characteristic humor and lucidity—in scholarship and poetry, as well as in all her sharply-etched, complex articulations of life within implacable racism. Later, P B-R and friends agreed that the minister was probably making an entirely appropriate bid for his own stronger presence on campus: to be appointed to the Chancellor's recent, hastily assembled "diversity council" (which was likely to remain largely titular). This seemed futile. No official UC representatives were there; the only administrators present were the 2 highest ranking black men. Worse, should the administration assent to replace Anne's position, which was by no means guaranteed, whoever the department hired was almost certain to move to a nearby white suburb like her colleagues—becoming ever more alienated and eager to leave, permanently peripheral to San Diego's black community.

Early on, P B-R had scanned the nearly full auditorium (the obituary had just come out that morning in San Diego's paper) for Lou, Becky's son. At the social hall, they shared a long hug then some incredible soul food as Lou introduced his Chinese American fiancée; they had met at school, reportedly much to her family's horror. When Lou's sweet grandmother sat down, P B-R introduced himself as her daughter's friend, and Lou's three-time teacher; graciously she kept the conversation light. On the drive home, P B-R exclaimed how great it was to see Lou accomplishing precisely what he had set out for: to teach high school English and coach football at his local alma mater. Amazingly, despite everything that had remained unsaid, the service still functioned exactly as they should and almost never do, the trio gratefully concurred: cohering an indelible, multi-dimensional portrait of Anne as unique and utterly irreplaceable; bridge, translator, keenly incisive commentator—to family, community, students, friends, colleagues, to virtually everybody who knew her.

Rae and John had never seen Lou before: of course, it would have been redundant to bring up to the highly appreciative pair P B-R's own dutifully suppressed pangs of lust. Happily, P B-R had developed a rapport with Lou before ever discovering he was Becky's son. He reminded them of the conversation in his office a few years back, on the last day of classes: Lou and another black student he knew from high school were discussing the possibility of teaching. Hoping to get into the Master's program without all the ed. requirements, Lou claimed to have some pull because Anne was his godmother. A surprised P B-R responded that he and Anne used to be very close, but she seemed to have withdrawn from almost everything since her friend Becky died. "That was my mother," Lou replied evenly. Suddenly, P B-R saw Becky's face transposed onto Lou's; he told Lou that, apologizing for staring. P B-R felt like he was having an acid flashback (which had rarely happened before, nor had he taken acid for over a decade). His mind was blown for several days: shocked into recognizing the longevity and complexity of his own roots in San Diego, despite baleful negativity about the place, as well as genuine wanderlust.

On the drive home, the trio dissected who and what was absent, and unspoken, at the services—exactly what everyone else must have been talking about right then. First and foremost, Anne's only child wasn't there because he was in prison; he was never mentioned, but every one of the pallbearers looked distinctly un-middle class and out of place among the richly dressed congregation. A number of people had spoken about Anne's steadfast devotion to her two grandsons, but nobody really went into how she had raised them since they were toddlers—never trusting one of the mothers in particular. Certainly, nobody articulated Anne's strong dying fears about these 13-year-olds' futures. Too sad to start in on her numerous illnesses and frustrations with Kaiser (and pointless, since Rae was also on Kaiser); Anne was so private that nobody had thought to intervene with connections to bigshot oncologists at the medical school until way too late.

Generally, in recent years there was profound isolation, bitter alienation from the department (combined with deep loyalty). P B-R was so thankful they had bonded in their 30's, when Anne was happier, doing her finest work—his experience and image of her were starkly different from those who'd met her later. They had admired and critiqued each other's manuscripts. Anne was key to P B-R collecting a series of interviews with local black residents on how the civil rights movement had affected their lives, for his So-Cal arts/literary magazine—Anne's own interview with Becky and family members was almost unbearably poignant to reread now. P B-R had been involved in civil rights demonstrations in the east in high school and college, leading into anti-war activism. Anne had always praised such organizing efforts, feeling uneasy about her life being too centered around the school.

After a much delayed and greatly needed crying bout at home, P B-R deliberately retreated back into research, typically more comfortable chasing theoretical geese and glad-handing inky information. He read that each generation after 1800 had reduced the number of its children, so that by the 19th century's end the nation's birthrate had been cut in half, from an average family size of more than seven children to fewer than four. In 1798, Thomas Malthus, an Anglican clergyman, had begun publishing postulates on the potential conflict between unrestrained population growth and the finite nature of the world's food supply. In 1821, the British liberal, John Stuart Mill, had written in the *Encyclopedia Brittanica* of the need to find more practical means of preventing contraception.

Fertility had obviously been inversely correlated with income, education, and job status, Margaret Sanger's own family experience being exemplary. Once Charles Goodyear successfully vulcanized rubber in 1837, a domestic industry developed in rubber condoms, which supplanted much more expensive ones made from the internal membranes of sheep and other animals. A dozen reusable condoms of allegedly high quality was advertised at $9 in 1847, at $5 in 1865, and at $1.50 in a Chicago mail order catalog from the 1880s. However, the annual average income of a working man in midcentury was only $600. During Margaret's childhood, abortions were also common and dangerous. Abortifacient properties were attached to chemicals like morphine and tannin, and to such plants as tulips, yarrow, milkweed, or rosemary, whose capacity to alter the estrogen and progesterone levels necessary to female reproduction had been scientifically confirmed.

Although fascinating, this vein of inquiry left P B-R no closer to being reconciled to life in San Diego, and certainly not to death there (naturally, of the most exceptional individuals). So he tried to conjure a more fulfilling "lifestyle": somehow meeting exciting new people—creative, intellectual, compassionate and witty, just like P B-R's friends!—in particular, hot and sane young black men (at least into their mid-thirties). After all, San Diego *is* a major urban center: doubtless, considerably less than half the population are monstrous rednecks, with another goodly chunk of homeless wrecks. Yet add in significant sectors of drunken urban cowboys, obsessive gym fanatics, earnest engineers, and crazed crystal freaks, and how many fractions, or factions, could be left? (He jingled his conceptual cage for good luck, or a good laugh.)

7.
OYSTERS, ANYONE?

Margaret Sanger's liberated sexuality was of a piece with the rest of her life. (After Noah died, Margaret's last casual love affair, with Hobson Pittman, a successful landscape painter twenty-one years younger, lasted six years and included many romantic trips back East and to Europe.) Margaret had the fantastic and impressive ability to manipulate the environment, wresting from it exactly what she needed: a canny strategist who frequently changed tactics over many decades of struggle. Of course, the Catholic church persisted as the most implacable enemy. But, it was difficult even to negotiate among her supporters' varied and often contradictory agendas: eugenicists and Social Darwinists, the medical establishment, feminists and other progressives.

Once Margaret fixed on the goal of building a national coalition of independent, not-for-profit birth control clinics (based on the medical model existing in Holland), she quickly recognized the necessity of garnering broad, mainstream publicity and support. She attempted to distance herself from her own infamous radical past, while still maintaining strong friendships with activists such as Elizabeth Gurley Flynn, Bill Haywood and Agnes Smedley (to whom Noah also sent money from time to time, including paying for her psychoanalysis). Assiduously courting and associating with prominent philanthropists and socialites, journalists, scientists, intellectuals, civic and health organization officials, politicians and world leaders tended to confer respectability on Margaret.

When she organized the First American Birth Control Conference at the Plaza Hotel in New York in 1921, for example, the list of sponsors featured Winston Churchill and Theodore Dreiser; guest speakers at the Town Hall opening, which the police shut down, were Harold Cox, a former member of the British Parliament and editor of the erudite *Edinburgh Review* and Mary Shaw, a popular Broadway actress and prominent supporter of women's causes. During the raid, Margaret, who was ordinarily "well-spoken and quietly attractive," remained effectively serene and poised, carrying a bouquet of long-stemmed roses as the police led her away. Just as the *New York Times* began commenting on her subversive past, media attention shifted to Juliet Rublee's arrest, in protest of the Town Hall raid.

Chesler believes that it was relatively easy for Margaret to shrug off her own youthful radicalism for a strategy of political accommodation due to her "distinct ambivalence toward her father's political beliefs." Deeply admiring his radical convictions, she frequently quoted Michael Higgins' admonition that the only obligation of his children was "to leave the world a better place"; but Margaret also "thrived unabashedly on success and could never tolerate a losing cause." Michael's persistent and inebriated radical discourse kept his family poor, as his wife's frugal, propertied family had predicted. Anne Higgins, Margaret's mother, suffered from chronic tuberculosis, with a cough so severe that she often had to brace herself against a wall to regain composure; emaciated, Anne died of consumption at age 50.

Still, whitewashing Margaret's image was hardly easy. For starters, she had been at the heart of the most famous and successful labor dispute of her day: the textile workers strike of 1912 at Lawrence, Massachusetts. She was asked by Wobbly organizers to lead a well-staged and highly publicized evacuation of workers' children from the strife-torn town to New York City. 22,000 people, most of them foreign born, were out of work, and the humanitarian tactic played brilliantly as sympathetic families in New York took in the forlorn children. The favorable newspaper coverage so enraged local authorities that they used billy clubs to prevent Elizabeth Gurley Flynn from leading a second contingent of children out of town.

This violence, in which strikers were viciously beaten in front of their children, provoked an investigation in Washington, attended by Helen Taft, the president's wife, and Alice Roosevelt, the former president's daughter, who came to hear the testimony of "the nurse from New York," as she was billed. Margaret's portrayal of the children of wool workers who in the cold of winter were without warm clothes made national headlines as a "remarkable exposition of capitalist brutality" and helped the strike to be favorably resolved. The results were not as positive, however, in Hazeltown, Pennsylvania a month later, when Margaret was arrested twice for trying to prevent workers from entering a silk factory which the Wobblies had not successfully organized.

For awhile, IWW successes led to their affiliation with the Socialist Party. Under the "elegiac national leadership" (as Chesler puts it) of Eugene Debs, the Party had polled almost 6 percent of the total vote in 1912, and elected more than 1,000 Socialists to office, including hundreds of aldermen and councilmen, 56 mayors, and a U.S. Congressman; Debs himself received a staggering 900,000 votes as the Party's presidential candidate. Debs was known for his ardent support of women's rights, and in 1908 what had long been a tradition of independent Socialist women's clubs was incorporated directly into the national party machinery.

But the Party quickly expelled Haywood and others whose top priority wasn't the electoral process, and who continued to advocate direct action. Margaret, along with most of the left wing of the Party, resigned in protest. She made the tabloids soon afterwards by leading a delegation of stylishly attired women in fancy cars down to the Bowery where they distributed reduced price meal tickets which they had reprinted in large numbers that Child's restaurant chain was giving away as a promotion.

When the organizers, nineteen-year-old anarchist Carlo Tresca and Frank Tannenbaum (who later became a distinguished history professor at Columbia University) implemented a more controversial tactic of forming bands of homeless people into roving "street armies" that demanded shelter in churches throughout the city, Tannenbaum was arrested for breaking and entering a church, ultimately spending a year in jail. His associate, Becky Edelsohn, was also arrested, and went on a well-publicized hunger-strike. Margaret left *The Call*, and in 1914 started her own newspaper, *The Woman Rebel*, which closely followed Becky Edelsohn's case.

Margaret's paper took the Wobblies' slogan, "NO GODS NO MASTERS," as its banner head. She had unsuccessfully approached the feminist group Heterodoxy to sponsor *The Woman Rebel*, since Margaret shared with the elite membership, including Charlotte Perkins Gilman, Crystal Eastman, and Henrietta Rodman, a disdain for a narrow suffragist focus, as well as for the factionalism and sexism of the left. Max Eastman endorsed the paper in *The Masses*, and Margaret raised money through subscriptions instead. But Eastman condescendingly accused Margaret of extremism and of falling into "that most unfeminine of errors—the tendency to cry out when a quiet and contained utterance is indispensable."

With Emma Goldman sounding the neo-Malthusian battle cry, the first issue of *The Woman Rebel* critiqued liberalism, and stressed economic independence for women. Margaret announced an upcoming series for girls 14 to 17 concerning their "natural impulses and feelings." Like Margaret Fuller and her close friend, Lydia Maria Child, editor of *the National Anti-Slavery Standard*, in the previous century, Margaret Sanger was a committed, lifelong advocate for prostitutes. *The Woman Rebel* vowed to "circulate among prostitutes, to voice their wrongs, to expose the police prosecution which hovers over them." Although *The Woman Rebel* was originally conceived as a vehicle to challenge the Comstock laws, as her trial date drew near, particularly Edelsohn's situation influenced Margaret to leave the country (with a fake passport in the name of Bertha Watson).

When Margaret returned to the U.S. the following year, the climate had turned more favorable for birth control, as she'd hoped. *Harper's Weekly*, the country's foremost popular intellectual forum, ran an exhaustive series on it, and the fledgling *New Republic* took up the much-heralded cause. William Sanger was on trial—he chose 30 days in jail rather than pay a $150 fine—which received sustained attention from the *New*

York Times. Further, a national coalition was emerging to support a constitutional amendment for women's suffrage which was finally achieved in 1920, so women's energies could be mobilized in other directions.

Margaret's sons, Stuart and Grant, viewed her departure to England as symptomatic of their chronic neglect; Margaret was also periodically ill with lingering tuberculosis nodules. With Noah's money, she dispatched both sons to exclusive prep schools, then to Harvard, and ultimately medical school. But, like their father, William Sanger, they suffered depression: Stuart, a poor student who repeated a grade in Europe with tutors, didn't start supporting himself till he was over 40. In 1953, Grant's first major depression led to a futile confrontation with Margaret, and to quitting his lucrative private practice in surgery.

Margaret was front page news again in 1916, when the police shut down the first birth control clinic in the nation which she had opened in a storefront tenement on Amboy Street in Brooklyn's Brownsville section, serving 464 recorded clients during several weeks. Handbills in English, Yiddish and Italian advertised the clinic while promoting the benefits of contraception over abortion. Two associates were also arrested, including Margaret's sister, Ethel Byrne, a registered nurse at Mt. Sinai Hospital, whose subsequent, media-saturated hunger strike occasioned a rally at Carnegie Hall, attended by 3,000 people, mostly women: newspapers noted a sharp contrast between the poor, working women and the "richly dressed" society types.

When Margaret and Fania Mindell were arrested by a plainclothes policewoman, Chesler comments that she "threw all caution to the wind, betraying her radical roots." The *Brooklyn Daily Eagle* described Margaret's "towering rage. 'You dirty thing,' she shrieked. 'You are not a woman. You are a dog!...and you have two ears to hear me too!'" According to the story, the two women were then "half-dragged, half carried" to a patrol wagon, defiantly followed by a gaggle of Brownsville women. Arraigned and released on $500 bail, they chose to reap the publicity value of remaining overnight in a cold, vermin-infested jail.

Though Margaret managed all publicity much like an old-fashioned Wobbly, her choice of Jonah Goldstein as counsel reflected a new political savvy. A young, liberal Democrat who had grown up on the Lower East Side under the tutelage of Lillian Wald, he began his political life as an aide to Al Smith, then majority leader of the New York State Assembly. Goldstein became a distinguished judge and family law theorist. Unable to win Margaret the jury trial which she wanted, Goldstein did get one virulent anti-birth control judge, who had previously convicted William Sanger, removed from the three-man panel that heard the case.

The prosecution accused Ethel Byrne of intending "to do away with the Jews" by dispensing contraception in an immigrant ghetto: she was sentenced to one month's imprisonment on Blackwell's Island. Newspapers throughout the country repeated Ethel's vow to undertake a hunger strike in the manner of the British suffragists, and "to die, if need be, for my sex." A farewell dinner of turkey and "plenty of ice cream" sustained the theatrics on the eve of her incarceration. The national wire services went wild when the New York City corrections commissioner decided, after four days, to begin forcible feeding of the prisoner through a tube inserted in the esophagus, for the first time in U.S. penal history. The usually sedate *New York Times* carried the story on its front page for four days in a row.

Margaret's lifetime of arduous organizing continued to yield many victories, incremental and cumulative: the most enduring ones coming well into old age. Her legislative reform campaigns were aimed mainly at allowing doctors (at first she included midwives) to prescribe contraceptives: an approach deriving from a vision of the socialized public health system that Havelock Ellis had introduced Margaret to in England and which she had observed in Holland, where doctors and nurses had been dispensing contraceptives since 1881. Margaret also controlled prestigious journals, such as the *Birth Control Review*. (When Agnes Smedley was made its editor, newly released from jail, at war's end, having been charged under the Sedition Act, an article appeared calling for a 5-year "birth strike" to prevent the unchecked reproduction of a "future crop of wage slaves.")

In 1936, Margaret pursued *United States v. One Package Containing 120, more or less, Rubber Pessaries to Prevent Conception*, the court case which resulted in birth control being exempted from the federal Comstock laws. As it turned out, it wasn't until the historic *Griswold v. Connecticut* decision of 1965 that the private use of contraceptives by married Americans was established as an inherent constitutional right. In 1970, Congress finally rewrote the federal Comstock laws removing the label of obscenity from contraception; two years later, the Supreme Court extended the right of contraceptive practice to the unmarried.

Also in 1965, as part of Lyndon Johnson's War on Poverty, the new Office of Economic Opportunity and various Planned Parenthood affiliates developed pilot projects to bring contraceptive services to married indigent women. Only one major condition for this initiative was set by OEO administrator Sargent Shriver: there be absolutely no publicity. Margaret died before these fledgling efforts were expanded in 1967, when Congress authorized the historic Title X Amendment to the Foreign Assistance Act, designating $35 million for family planning assistance to foreign governments, United Nations agencies and private non-profit organizations; amendments to the Social Security Act stipulated that no less than 6% of funds for Maternal and Child Health Services be spent on domestic family planning.

Happily, Margaret did live to see another of her greatest achievements come to pass. She was over 80 when the team of doctors she had long been encouraging marketed the oral, anovulant birth control pill. In 1946, Margaret had become despondent on her two-week national tour of family planning clinics: "millions of women were still in need of what she identified with great prescience...as a 'birth control pill.'" Contraceptive technology had not advanced much since she sponsored the American Birth Control League's inaugural Conference in 1921 which reviewed evidence for the success of the IUD (then made of silver and gold). More convinced than ever that Planned Parenthood, for whose leadership she had utter contempt, only cared to reach the middle classes, Margaret rallied a group of supporters to petition its board to endow a fund whose sole purpose was research into cheaper and simpler methods.

In 1953, two intrepid scientists who'd been denied tenure at Harvard formed the Worcester Foundation for Experimental Biology. Building on the earlier discovery and isolation of estrogen, and subsequent synthesis of progesterone, using the roots of a wild Mexican yam in 1942, Gregory Goodwin Pincus and Hudson Hoagland continued to examine various scientific principles necessary for the manufacture of synthetic hormone contraceptives. When Margaret first met Pincus in 1951, she immediately introduced him to an old friend, Katherine McCormick. One of the first two women to receive a degree in science from MIT, when Katherine McCormick's young husband (heir to the International Harvester Company fortune) suffered a schizophrenic breakdown from which he never recovered, she was forced to find a new focus for her life in philanthropy. McCormick died in 1967, at age 92, having given the Worcester Foundation more than $2 million, and leaving them another million in her will. By the 1970s, close to 50 million women worldwide were using oral contraceptives.

8.
INQUIRING PERIPATETICS
WANT TO KNOW

Inquisitive Peripatetic awakens at noon to the bustle and clamor of the mercurial, LA marketplace. Here, athletic individuals consume with purpose: shiny (self-)images proliferate like weeds of dubious beauty. Costly goodies sprout in a veritable fount of balm. Money talks, nobody walks. Oxymorons can casually command a pretty penny! Provocative packages come in virtually all licking colors; flavorful foods flow freely like fabled, fruity fortunes.

Nor are musky oxen sold here; neither frankincense and myrrh (save for the short-lived, chi-chi, tax write-off shoppe). Macrame is in short demand; moose is still suspiciously seasonal. Mainly, it is silky flesh, satiny sinks, slinky leather trusses, relaxed cotton frocks, radiant rouge rayon, high concept sex/violence plastique wear which goose the golden gander's eggs, and gild all sorts of wayward Millies.

Everyone has a fixed place at the great/good slaughterhouse/fair: determined randomly and more or less firmly at birth, according to family money and position. That is not immediately evident, from the seeming ease and freedom of movement of certain sectors of the population. In the ragged outskirts of the marketplace, however—regions which used to be called the inner city—economic exigencies are stark, out where skins are dark, and jobs are scarce as pickled pomegranates.

The California public at large appears wholly unaware of the horrific ramifications of poverty, and vastly indifferent to the lives of the marginal, homeless, the addicted, in their city-street-to-jail-sans-rehab, dead-end, penitentiary loops. Resolutely yet inattentively, vacant voters validate vicious racist initiatives, such as denying education and emergency medical care to "illegals." They know who to blame it on, all right—though the actual nature of "it" eludes them like a greased salami.

Citizens grimly cling to their own ignorant bliss: to them, suburbs gleam like an alluring dead animal. But will the twin bugaboos of familial violence and drugs beat down their carefully hand-crafted doors, too? No wonder cool observers, such as Peripatetic Book-Reviewer, liken these good burg(h)ers to crazed coyotes mistaking vodka for clear water. Mesmerists first, then memorists—murky mannerists of memory, maybe—they wear money like a hog. (Evidently, Peripatetic Book-Reviewer prefers to mentally inhabit the past.)

Beautiful, slinking bodies are the order of the city's workaday, sassing their way through streets and sheets. Oddly, bus stops ooze unctuously. The gym offers a literal lathe: turning 24-7, to create so many *fine* consorts for the wealthy, who drive Jaguar convertibles around crowded areas, rarely deigning to glance at prosaic passersby. Seeing themselves as having the power of rich gazelles who could purchase a small dukedom, such drivers, assesses Peripatetic B-R, are really more typically So-Cal than LA, which is characterized by nothing if not a certain frank, and anarchic, mercantile friendliness.

Happily, people at all levels, everywhere in LA (sometimes even among the wealthy and their would-be courtesans) often resist being defined by commodity/consumer positioning in the macro-marketplace. Technical skills are consistently in demand in Hollywood: by day, many ply their trades, dogged, graceful, sustained by a proud expertise, and chiefly by good-natured, co-worker camaraderie. Traversing the mercifully balmy city are musicians, video artists, fledgling stars, painters, writers, animators, activists, computer graphics whizballs.

Unconfined, on some nights anyway, P B-R voraciously craves conversation with eccentric friends: journalists, writers, teachers, several from the art institute which just hired him for a semester of pedagogy and persuasion courses, and, hopefully, will continue to save P B-R from San Diego! (At first, obsessively needing to talk about Anne's death: very hard to describe its impact, since unusual and talented people are fairly abundant in LA, and any one individual is much less crucial to the sanity and vitality of the whole environment.) The gang delves into tempting taste treats at the inexpensive Peruvian, or sassy Sri Lankan restaurant, only a short drive away; flocking to subcultural events of all kinds, ruminating, evaluating, salivating, and primarily laughing until it finally stops hurting. Surely *not* entirely atypical urban dwellers: many people must be considerably more aware of galloping, lethal racism than skeptical P B-R usually suspects.

Itinerant scholar, teacher, writer, researcher and book reviewer, Peripatetic One copes with the marketplace adequately, insofar as it needs his rather antiquated skills of articulation with élan (as his business card claims): his resume is a veritable user's manual for Cyclops with shy amanuensis. (Rightly, he should be called Itinerant Academic, but P B-R can't bear to think he's been squeezed into dependence on those particular hallowed halls.) P B-R enjoys an imaginary journey, definitely not a virtual one: foolishly fancying that his technophobia places him in closer mental proximity to choice paragons from earlier ages.

Skimming vibrantly through piles of books, at least he's frequently diverted from stratified monkeyshines going on right under his growing nose. Obviously, this is not *quite* the same Peripatetic Book-Reviewer who previously manifested: you may recall that modest, piquant social commentator didn't wish to call attention to himself. Such change of heart and groin erupted mostly from gaping cognitive dissonance as he studied the 19th and early 20th century America. Yearning expanded for a robust era when hope seemed plausible, or minimally "native moral indignation"(as one chatty critic recently described the estimable *The Masses*, pre-WWI Greenwich Village, Socialist arts and literary magazine, and major Comstock casualty).

P B-R has researched the hideous saga of industrialization—abiding, widespread poverty, labor's prolonged, out-and-out class warfare, disastrous infant mortality rate—so it's not accurate to say he wishes to have lived in an earlier period. It's simply that P B-R prefers living then *now*. When virulent racism, crippling poverty and addiction have become personified in the infamous, three-strikes law: fatalistic gallows.

Stupidly, he feels the best way to reconcile himself to the present—having witnessed a mountain of exploitation, and way too many early deaths—is in cataloging catastrophic aspects of yesteryear, like influenza epidemics, or the tuberculosis which carried off Margaret Sanger's 5-year-old daughter, Peggy, in 1915. Of course, Margaret Fuller died clutching her infant son, who was swept out of her arms in the end. She had already faced the deaths of two favorite five-year-olds, the Emersons' and Greeleys' sons. Both Margarets were from large families: two of Fuller's and one of Sanger's siblings died in childhood. In this, they were truly of their generations.

Margaret Sanger never wholly stopped mourning or feeling guilty; through the years, she kept an "imaginary landscape" in which Peggy grew to maturity, "untouched by harsh actuality and disillusion." Initially, guilt was exacerbated by her young sons' claims that Peggy never would have become so ill if their mother hadn't been away in England that year. On the anniversaries of Peggy's birth and death, Margaret always canceled her public appointments and mourned. Grant, who could barely remember the lone companion of his youth, regularly wrote or phoned his mother in this ritual.

A longtime atheist, Sanger began to study Rosicrucianism after Peggy's death: this fashionable mystical cult, which Havelock Ellis had introduced her to in London, advanced a regimen of private meditation to connect the individual to powers within the self derived from a supreme high force. Margaret accepted the premise that every individual possesses a "spark of divinity," which, her biographer writes, "gave a spiritual dimension to the doctrine of self-reliance she absorbed from such icons of secular American culture as Ralph Waldo Emerson and her father's hero, Robert Ingersoll."

The very last time the 83-year-old Margaret left her nursing home was a strangely auspicious visit to young Margaret Sanger, who had married her second cousin, Dom Marston; she had just given birth to her first child, a little girl they called Peggy. When her great-granddaughter was brought to her, Margaret became animated, repeating, "Peggy's come back. Peggy's come back." She then ran her hands over the infant's head to discern her personality from its shape and contour, as her father's phrenology books had instructed. The new baby had been born nearly forty-seven years to the day of little Peggy Sanger's death, when Margaret had actually believed she saw the light of Peggy's soul ascending to the heavens—during their imaginary conversations, Margaret fully anticipated that one day they would be reunited.

Despite her nonconforming radicalism, Margaret was part of a surprisingly large intellectual following among liberals and progressives well into the 1930s who assumed eugenic principles were compatible with a commitment to social welfare initiatives in education, health, and labor. From its outset in the late nineteenth century when Francis Galton, a cousin of Charles Darwin, called for the regulation of human reproduction, eugenics persisted as a force in the birth control movement. Just before he first met Margaret, Havelock Ellis had aligned himself with them by publishing *The Task of Social Hygiene*, which addressed the need for systematic prevention of social ills before they became problems. In one speech, Margaret bemoaned the burden of the "unfit" on productive members of the community. She then committed birth control to the creation of a "race of thoroughbreds," a phrase originally penned in the popular *Literary Digest*, by a progressive physician advocating state endowment of maternal and infant care clinics.

Both before and after World War I, eugenics became a popular craze in the country; in 1923, a national advocacy group, the American Eugenics Society, was founded, which sponsored sermon contests in churches and synagogues and "fitter family" contests at state fairs. (In 1928, the American Birth Control League rejected a proposal to join forces with this organization.) The great majority of American colleges and universities introduced courses in the subject. Even the young American Communist Party leader Norman Thomas voiced concern about the "alarming high birth rate of definitely inferior stock." Also endorsing eugenics was the prominent Russian anarchist theorist Peter Kropotkin, who influenced Emma Goldman, much as Ellis had Sanger and the writer Olive Schreiner. They all spoke against selective breeding, and racial stereotyping; nevertheless, it became increasingly difficult to separate their positions from the virulent race baiting which accompanied waves of anti-immigrant sentiment in the '20s and '30s.

What is more, nearly universal agreement was reached in the 1920s, on the propriety of 30 states enacting compulsory sterilization statutes for individuals carrying deficiencies believed to be inherited, such as mental retardation, insanity, or uncontrollable epilepsy. By 1930, California had sterilized 7,500 institutionalized dependents. Virginia's statute was, in fact, upheld by the United States Supreme Court in 1927. The majority opinion in the notorious *Buck v. Bell* case was written by Justice Oliver Wendell Holmes, Jr., with Louis Brandeis also voting in favor. (The lone dissent was from a Catholic, ostensibly opposed on moral grounds.) Although Holmes and Brandeis had built their reputations as liberal proponents of free speech, both were willing to sacrifice the rights of individuals who "sap the strength of the state," as Holmes put it. Arguing that collective social interests would take precedence in these instances, he wrote, "Three generations of imbeciles are enough."

Meanwhile, Peripatetic Book-Reviewer continues to ponder penning mordant articles on Margaret Fuller: perhaps Rio will host the next conference. (He muses that he might have a better shot at that Vancouver trip if he returns to writing about Budd Schulberg's novels, though he recalls preferring the screenplays.) Sitting down to contemplate his notes, a restless P B-R wonders: could he abandon his self-absorption long enough to truly tackle murky and martyred Margaret, not to mention even momentarily cease obsessive ranting about his own miserably debased time and place? At the moment, P B-R is in a furor over mundane yet mystifying memos and such.

Of course, it's not yet clear how much work to even try to get done, beyond finishing the Cunanan reviews—especially if P B-R is in LA only for the one semester. There's so much divine talking and hanging out to be accomplished, way too much business, *and* the presence of a longterm, if sporadic sex partner: James, ultra busy but currently (sort of) unattached. In San Diego, P B-R is used to conveniently separating friendship and sex—except, naturally, for becoming too emotionally involved with a few of the (semi-)hustlers he gets to know (typically, sexy and smart, black crystal addicts who are barely managing to stay out of prison) when James' company is touring, or when Mr. Mister is swooning over somebody new in LA.

Still, one glorious, sun-drenched if cloudy day, envisions P B-R, he may well rise to the saucy challenge, and whip out a taut and logical article on Fuller: San Diego has always been a great place to get work done. Funny, he can't quite remember if this particular gauntlet was originally flung down by himself or by a dull facsimile. In any case, he believes such confusion is significant: symptomatic of the first-wave, postwar baby boom generation, who consider themselves idealistic, despite everyday reality having long become transparently vicious, and their own buttressed vehicles steadily sinking or swimming down Dirty Lucre Lane.

Right off the bat, P B-R realizes he'll have to re-skim some of the biographical and biological surfaces, and make efficient, judicious use of indexes. However, he has confidence in his own cocky cogency, which he's sure any putative publisher or virile patron should find invaluable—*if* such a hapless chap is ever relocated. For now, Peripatetic Book-Reviewer recognizes that narratives simply stimulate readers' dusty doubts about the author's (if not their own) very existence. But he figures a theoretical precedent can inevitably be found or manufactured. Anyhow, in an ascendant stupor, he suddenly reckons this is somebody else's problem altogether; happily, P B-R forgets practically everything (not) in/sight.

Book 3
HIDING IN THE LIGHT

BAYARD RUSTIN: Troubles I've Seen
Jervis Anderson
University of California Press, 1998

LUSH LIFE: A Biography of Billy Strayhorn
David Hajdu
Granta Books, 1996

1.
ISSUING FORTH

The cold and brilliant (light) light is now flooding through the window. The glowing sky can be seen outside exactly as the tattered and bohemian prophets predicted long ago. The varied play of light seems to come not only from the window but from all sides: through the walls and the cracks in the cupboard, from the furniture. The unearthly producer, the set-designer, and the lighting specialist should remember that although the atmosphere of the birth chamber evidently changes, it most definitely suggests the mingled presence of terror and dignified beauty.

EMERGING: Bayard Rustin, major leader of two movements, worldwide pacifism, American civil rights. Brilliant strategist of civil disobedience, tireless and exacting organizer of demonstrations small to massive, this self-styled sophisticate with his cultivated British accent (and valuable collection of antique canes) sang gospel songs in a way that demolished then rearranged the known world. (Stage lights entirely disappear; lacy trees glow evenly.)

Openly gay at a time when only someone of the stature of his friend James Baldwin could get away with that, Rustin remained a leader behind the scenes, without a group or constituency. Master of praxis, Rustin moved with the cunning and savvy of a fine anarchist (he was far from that) troubleshooter, who knows precisely where to appear just when his skills are most urgently needed.

Rustin began public life as a Quaker deeply committed to the pacifist movement. Officially, he was shared at different times by several organizations: FELLOWSHIP OF RECONCILIATION; WAR RESISTERS LEAGUE; an original member of CORE which sponsored the first freedom ride, the Journey of Reconciliation in 1947 (whose results were largely symbolic and resulted in a 30-day stretch for Rustin on a North Carolina chain gang), and SCLC. Later, Rustin headed the A. Philip Randolph Institute and was nominal chairman of Social Democrats USA, when the Socialist Party split in 1972 (a minority faction led by Michael Harrington became the Democratic Socialists of America).

In 1956, Rustin was Director of the War Resisters League which gave him the first of many furloughs to go South: the Southern novelist Lillian Smith (*Strange Fruit*) had suggested to Martin Luther King, Jr. that Rustin be sent to help with the Montgomery bus strike.

As the only clergyman in Montgomery not enmeshed in dubious alliances with the white power structure, at 26, King had been thrust into the leadership of the boycott. Rustin's mission was to teach King how to put his somewhat sketchy academic knowledge (culled at Boston University's divinity school) of Gandhian civil disobedience into practice. One of the first lessons was to convince him to get rid of the gun he'd recently purchased after his home was bombed. (Later, King remarked about this period, "I had merely an intellectual understanding and appreciation of the position, with no firm determination to organize it.")

Although they had never met, Rustin's task was made easier by Coretta Scott King's warm reception; she had heard him lecture about being a conscientious objector for the Fellowship of Reconciliation, at her high school in Marion, Alabama in 1940. ("He became very close to us," Coretta Scott King recalled, "and was tremendously helpful to my husband.") Predictably, Rustin's presence in Montgomery caused great alarm, with the local press denouncing him as an "NAACP Communist organizer trained in Moscow."

Back in New York, 44-year-old Rustin continued organizing fundraisers—rallies at Madison Square Garden and elsewhere featured Tallulah Bankhead, Harry Belafonte and Duke Ellington—building support networks, and securing cars from Northern union workers to be sent South for use in the boycott. The success of the year-long bus boycott led to the birth of the Southern Christian Leadership Conference, under King's leadership, to promote non-violent direct action, as distinct from the NAACP's focus on federal legislation and challenging Jim Crow laws.

Throughout his close working alliance with King, there was widespread opposition to Rustin among more conservative black leaders, due to his sexual orientation, youthful radical affiliations, and the fact that he had been jailed for 28 months as a conscientious objector during the Second World War. In 1960, Adam Clayton Powell, Jr., who was currying favor with the Kennedys, forced SCLC to cancel civil disobedience planned for the Democratic national convention by threatening to publicly announce that King (a well-known womanizer) and Rustin were engaging in a homosexual liaison. Although a few years earlier King had asked Rustin to serve as SCLC's first associate director (which he turned down, wanting neither to work as an administrator nor move to Atlanta), King reacted to Powell's threats with an ominous silence, causing Rustin to resign from SCLC. In a statement published in the *New York Courier*, a weekly coming out of Harlem, Rustin explained:

> I cannot permit a situation to endure in which the best elements of the Negro leadership are attacked as a result of my relationship to them…Those who have worked with me during my twenty years in the movement know that I have never sought high position or special privilege, but have always made myself available to the call of the leadership. Twenty-two arrests in the North and South, including time on a North Carolina chain gang, in the course of fighting Jim Crow, are the recorded measure of my dedication, not to political power but to the ideals of our struggle. Nevertheless, Congressman Powell has suggested that I am an obstacle to his giving full, enthusiastic support to Dr. King. I want now to remove that obstacle.

Partly due to James Baldwin's aggressive defense, Rustin soon found himself back in King's inner circle, where he played a pivotal role by taking on (somewhat at the eleventh hour) the daunting task of organizing the historic 1963 march on Washington which culminated in the famous "I Have a Dream" speech. Swayed by A. Phillip Randolph's arguments that Rustin was the only man with the experience to get the job done, the black leadership ignored Strom Thurmond's vitriolic fulminating on Capitol Hill as well as objections by Roy Wilkins (who, like Whitney Young with the Urban League, wouldn't commit NAACP participation until civil disobedience had been ruled out). A week afterwards, on September 6, 1963, Rustin was featured on the cover of *Life*, standing alongside his mentor, A. Phillip Randolph, as architects of the march; he was referred to as "The Strategist Without a Movement," "The Lone Wolf of Civil Rights," "The Socrates of the Civil Rights Movement."

2.
POLITICAL ISSUES

Although the 1963 march was an unprecedented triumph, it didn't result in the Kennedy administration providing promised federal legislation. It also began to create new adversaries for Rustin among former allies from the more militant wing of the civil rights movement which felt silenced by the rally's accommodationist message. John Lewis, 25-year-old chairman of SNCC, had prepared an unsparing speech which Wilkins and others objected to. On the podium, A. Phillip Randolph convinced Lewis to excise words like "the masses" and "revolution," but Lewis' speech remained the most caustic delivered that day. There were no women speakers, for which Rustin was later criticized by Ella Baker and others. (Malcolm X., who had previously made negative remarks about the march, showed up in D.C., telling reporters, "Well, whatever black folks do, maybe I don't agree with it, but I'm going to be there, brother, because that's where I belong.")

Rustin's short-lived iconization began dissolving almost immediately, as the whole tenor of the country and the movement became more violent. A little more than a week after the *Life* cover, segregationists in Birmingham bombed a black church, killing four children and injuring many others. At a rally in Manhattan, James Baldwin urged a boycott of Christmas shopping, and Rustin called for a national nonviolent uprising, to form "a mountain of creative social confusion, by sitting in the streets, by disrupting the ability of government to finally operate." Rustin's biographer comments that "a hint of desperation in both proposals suggested that the tactics of nonviolence were unequal to those employed by its enemies." "The younger militants," he adds, "began to feel that the ethic of nonviolence had outlived its usefulness."

As the '60s bore on, Rustin's chief priority became coalition building, primarily with labor, in order to influence and extend Lyndon Johnson's domestic poverty programs. This alienated many of the younger black leaders, like Stokely Carmichael, who had formerly admired Rustin's radical agenda. (Carmichael and co-author Charles V. Hamilton devote a chapter of *BLACK POWER* to SNCC's critique of the limitations, and inherent historical contradictions of Rustin's strategy of coalition building with liberals, whose primary aim was not to reorientate and revamp society's basic structures—the only real potential for dealing with racism.) James Farmer commented, "Bayard has no credibility in the black community. His commitment is to labor, not the black man. His belief that the black man's problem is economic, not racist, runs counter to black community thinking." An early instance concerned the Freedom Democratic Party, which demanded to be seated as the democratically elected representatives of Mississippi to the 1964 national party convention, as opposed to the regular, all-white delegation. That was unacceptable to Johnson who proposed a compromise of 2 seats for the FDP; Rustin joined King, Roy Wilkins, James Farmer and others in unsuccessfully urging the FDP to accept this proposition.

Rustin sided with labor in New York City school board disputes, in a series of teacher strikes in 1967 and '68, about which black and hispanic community leaders complained bitterly that their children were the chief victims. In May '68, the administrator of an experimental board for community control, which had been set up earlier in the Ocean Hill-Brownsville district of Brooklyn, transferred a number of white teachers out of the local schools and hired black ones; the UFT called a strike. The only active black leader to back the union, Rustin was called an "Uncle Tom" and accused of supporting a move to neutralize an experiment in minority self-determination. Fervently opposing separatism, for awhile Rustin also injudiciously described burgeoning Black Studies programs on college campuses as an escape from rigorous academic training; he edited a collection of essays by writers like Roy Wilkins and the historian Vann Woodward who concurred with those disparaging ideas.

Rustin's position on Vietnam was particularly frustrating to an array of former friends and allies among Democratic Socialists and the radical pacifist movement (which he had recently abandoned as unviable, except as "personal witness to the truth as one sees it"). Rustin called for a negotiated and systematic settlement of the Vietnam War while David Dellinger and Michael Harrington, for instance, were seeking immediate and unconditional American withdrawal from Indochina. (Harrington had come around to apologetically viewing his former pronouncements—that the U.S. could afford both "butter and guns," that the Vietnam War needn't be pursued at the expense of poor people—as a grave error.) Rustin's stance was in line with the labor movement. AFL-CIO president George Meany (who used to consider Rustin a dangerous radical) was an ardent hawk, and his union served as a conduit for millions of dollars of aid from the State Dept. to anticommunist unions in South Vietnam. At its December, 1966 national convention, the AFL-CIO delegates voted nearly unanimously for a resolution supporting the Johnson administration's policies in Vietnam.

Most of his former allies regarded moderates like Rustin as hardline anticommunists, insensitive to the North Vietnamese struggle for national liberation and therefore in tacit agreement with the aims of American war policy. Although Rustin was only one of several black leaders like Roy Wilkins and Ralph Bunche, the highest ranking black in the United Nations Secretariat, who were critical when Martin Luther King, Jr. publicly opposed the war in 1967 (denouncing "my own government" as "the greatest purveyor of violence in the world today"), detractors identified Rustin as the main opponent of King's new approach of linking civil rights with other urgent problems.

Rustin *was* a hard-line anticommunist, having been a member of the Young Communist League in the early '40s, sent to City College of New York to recruit students. He claimed to have played a leading role in the communist takeover of CCNY's student senate, campus newspaper and later the American Student Union—a nursery for some of the left-wing intellectuals who entered American public life during and immediately after World War II. Viewing the Communist Party as the only predominantly white organization which was dedicated to fighting racism, Rustin was ecstatic in 1941 to be assigned to organize and lead a campaign against desegregation in the armed services. But that was quickly cancelled when the Nazis invaded the Soviet Union, and he was told the fight for desegregation would be disruptive to the military machine. Disillusioned, Rustin quit YCL, saying that he now realized, "the communists' primary concern was not with the black masses but with the global objectives of the Soviet Union."

In 1965, Staughton Lynd, a professor of history at Yale and national antiwar spokesperson, wrote and circulated "An Open Letter to Bayard Rustin," following this with an attack in the pages of *Liberation*, a publication which Rustin had once edited, calling him a "labor lieutenant of capitalism" in "coalition with the Marines." Later, Lynd explained that he had singled out Rustin as a leading advocate of the strategy of working within the Democratic party chiefly because "Bayard has for so long inspired myself and others of my generation as a passionate practitioner of radical civil disobedience and nonviolent revolution."

During the mid '60s, A. Philip Randolph came up with the concept of the Freedom Budget, which became Rustin's focus too: basically, it called for a living wage for all Americans, as well as an enormous expansion of the billion dollar budget that Lyndon Johnson had just set aside for his new, high profile war on poverty. In an excellent biography of Michael Harrington (former Catholic Worker, longtime socialist friend and ally of Rustin whose impactful book *The Other America* was the bible of the antipoverty movement), Maurice Isserman suggests that Randolph's Freedom Budget "was a hopeless cause from the moment it was first proposed" and that it was an error to attempt to use it as the centerpiece of the activists' domestic strategy. Randolph's proposal called for 10 billion dollars a year to be spent on domestic poverty programs, with a ten-year campaign to expend more than $180 billion. But by 1966, Johnson was focussing on Vietnam. Legislators and Johnson himself had lost interest in his own domestic programs, which he had never envisioned enlarging; the term war on poverty soon vanished entirely from the White House rhetoric.

Rustin consistently acted in solidarity with the American Jewish community, partly because they had been a major force in bankrolling King's campaigns (his friend, and King's close adviser, Stanley Levinson, a wealthy attorney and political intellectual, was identified by the FBI as a dangerous communist) which angered many black leaders. In 1966, he chaired the Committee on the Rights of Soviet Jewry. In 1972, he was the only black leader to attend a memorial service in Manhattan for Israeli athletes murdered by Arab terrorists at the Munich Olympic Games. At the invitation of Elie Weisel, Rustin chaired the U.S. Holocaust Memorial Council (later, he was among a group that nominated Weisel for the Nobel Peace Prize). On visits to Israel, Rustin established a close personal friendship with Golda Meir; in 1976, Hebrew University funded a scholarship in his name.

Rustin was appalled by black anti-Semitism, and argued that it was greatly exaggerated, citing an ADL study (an organization which frequently honored him): "Negroes, when asked whether or not they would rather rent, buy from, work for, or owe money to Jews or other white people, chose Jews by a very high percentage." "What Bayard liked about Jews," his old pacifist comrade Roy Finch said, "was how well organized and unified they were. He thought that Jews used every bit of the power and influence they had. And he wanted blacks to do the same...in coalition with other forces."

3.
PERIPATETIC BOOK-REVIEWER NESTLING

Peripatetic Book-Reviewer was thankful that he hadn't tried to do everything on the one long weekend in LA. Going through multitudes of Kathy's boxes had been quite enough: literally hundreds of them stacked randomly on top of each other in Matias' huge two-story garage. Even hauling them down to open them was a major effort. At least last summer, when P B-R, Carla and Amy went through the million boxes of books, it wasn't so physically exhausting. And what a payoff! To come upon almost in the very last box the wondrous cache of her final manuscripts (destined for the archives at Duke) whose existence they had all assumed, but nobody knew about for sure.

Those boxes had been sealed for over 3 years, since Kathy had them packed and stored in London when she left for an American tour. (Getting them shipped to Matias' took more than a year until he could prove that her intention was to move back to San Francisco, thus probate shouldn't go through the British courts.) Kathy must have had somebody just wrap and pack every single thing in the apartment: stained and torn clothes mixed with expensive designer dresses; hundreds of shoes and boots many of which looked unworn; numerous leather sets for motorcycle riding; more varieties of sex toys than P B-R ever knew existed; broken appliances and new kitchen ware; many elegant oriental rugs, tea sets and dishes; chairs and kitchen table; empty, half-used and unopened jars of skin cream and bottles of vitamins. The pay-off there, aside from finally dealing with this, being the unexpected photographs that Kathy had saved—some from childhood of her mother (infamous in the annals of literature). Most astonishing was the wedding photo from when she and Acker got married after her sophomore year, right before they moved to San Diego: she looked so young and infinitely sweet. Nobody could even recognize her except P B-R who knew Kathy then.

Amy was the only person P B-R could have done this with, who had the right combination of black humor and unapologetic feeling: moving swiftly, deftly deciding what to put aside for Kathy's friends—stuffed animals, skull rings, photos—not to mention being able to resolutely ignore the awful, asthmatic-inducing, moldy clothes and cold garage. Estimating quantities, Amy arranged for OUT OF THE CLOSET, the AIDS thrift store, to pick everything up. P B-R and Amy talked several times later that weekend; both were recuperating. Amy sadly and somewhat obsessively inferring Kathy's state of mind when she was having everything packed; how sick was she then? Did she ever admit that the alternative "natural" treatments weren't working? Excoriating herself for not being more forceful about Kathy's going through radiation after her mastectomy, though they both knew she had been intractable.

What a mistake it would have been to schedule this on the same weekend Paul was going to be in LA. When they were younger, that wasn't so rare: both were more or less bicoastal for a decade or so after they graduated from Brandeis in the late '60s. But Paul hadn't been out to California for years, and it seemed like forever since P B-R felt he could afford a real trip to New York. Hopefully by the time Paul does arrive, Peripatetic Book-Reviewer will have stopped this random, apparently unprovoked crying: not even thinking about Kathy in particular, or so many dead friends (different from his customary tears at sentimental old movies or almost anything on tv about race). Responding to P B-R's email from San Diego, Amy confirmed she was in a similar state back in New York.

Clearly, he needed to start a new writing project—teaching was going well, and his schedule was mercifully light. He had turned down two book reviews, hoping to become engaged in something more serious, maybe about Baldwin's essays, having recently taught *The Evidence Of Things Not Seen* again, a remarkable pinnacle of 20th century American nonfiction: a kind of anthropological investigation into the Atlanta child murders in which each assumption and statement of all players (especially Baldwin's own) is scrupulously interrogated and contextualized. Reading Baldwin's biography had briefly led to the unimaginable—trying to conceive of what it felt like for Baldwin and his urbane friend Bayard Rustin to be openly gay black men in that era. P B-R did know that the pair had much in common: sophisticated intellectuals who enjoyed late-night philosophical conversations over drinks, both were expert at leading mass meetings and enjoyed swaying a crowd with their words. Not only were both gay, of course, but they were also illegitimate; Baldwin used to joke about their being "black bastard queers" (though they allowed no one else to call them that).

Just at that time, his copy of *California Educator*, the teachers' union magazine, came in the mail. There was an unusually interesting article about Layle Lane, a black teacher, union activist and Socialist Party candidate for New York state office who reportedly had a profound influence on the young Bayard Rustin: appalled at his communist affiliations, she helped steer him into the camp of A. Phillip Randolph who was organizing an all black march on Washington for the desegregation of the military, cancelled only when Franklin D. Roosevelt agreed to issue an executive order banning discrimination in defense industries. On the same day, P B-R got an email about a union meeting to update lecturers on contract negotiations. Always a believer in synchronicity, or paying close attention to coincidence (at least since his LSD decade), P B-R thought it might behoove him to be reading or writing about unionism now.

The meeting disabused him of that notion, however (unless he wished to perfect the art of diatribe). He had hoped that medical benefits would be a featured agenda item. Periodically, P B-R obsessed about his own lack of benefits, due to moving around so much as well as to the lame union contracts at the UC and Cal State schools where he tended to work: basically, he paid for major medical and tried not to go to the doctor. On the occasional semester when he was teaching enough courses in one place to qualify for health coverage, P B-R would dutifully get check-ups, blood and cholesterol tests, playing the standard numbers game of someone his age.

Eleven people showed up at the meeting, which was scheduled to last one hour: 7 lecturers (out of hundreds on campus) and 4 union representatives, each of whom spoke at some length about their own most poignant and gratifying moments as organizers. When one woman asked rather quietly, "Shouldn't we be concerned that there are only 7 people here?" the barrage of testimonies to unionism came even thicker, followed by inspirational tales about the glory days of the AFL-CIO itself. "There's strength in unity," cried one organizer, as if addressing a slightly precocious 6th grade class. Instead of discussing strategy relevant to the low turnout, they referred obliquely to upcoming mass actions at which other unions, all members of the Central Labor Council, would swiftly leap to our aid.

Incredibly, one official suggested that lecturers should save their students' thank-you notes as evidence that they really do deserve to teach additional courses. Scant mention was made of health benefits. When P B-R explained his own situation, which involved being hired on and off for decades, typically at a level that made him ineligible for any benefits, and with no credit for cumulative service because it wasn't "unbroken," a negotiator expressed surprise at some of those rules. Two hours later, P B-R and his 2 friends left totally disheartened, angry at the waste of time, quite convinced they'd "fucking better stay healthy." They exchanged bemused remarks about past thank you's they'd received from various semi-deranged students.

Hopefully, this wouldn't trigger off a mini period of depression and anxiety about the future. P B-R often reasoned with himself: while enjoying a peripatetic lifestyle (including intellectually, by not sticking to one genre or field) certainly had its inherent limitations, it was a choice he'd made long ago—simply to follow his own proclivities—so he shouldn't whine about the consequences. And the fact was he still liked teaching, plus he had some mobility (i.e. could get out of San Diego more or less regularly). He sometimes thought about trying to maneuver into a career situation now, in his early-ish 50's, while it was vaguely possible, though already long out of the question in teaching where he was indelibly marked as reliable part-timer: semi-jack-of-all-trades—not as cheap as he used to be! Occasional freelance journalism or editing was fine, but in fact, there was no job which P B-R could stand full time, especially in Hollywood-saturated LA, where he'd prefer to be. In any case, P B-R doubted that the liaison with Himself could survive their actual living in the same city—he definitely preferred James as intermittent lover to friend.

To ward off depression, P B-R had recourse to a more or less standard bag of tricks: in the past, revolving around drugs and sex, now mostly entailing movies and dinner with friends (and sex). Or rereading something wonderful from the 19th century, of course (possibly early 20th), like *Villette* or *What Maisie Knew*: books having always been first line of defense in alienated childhood. Once he becomes depressed, 19th century novels remain the sine qua non—as they are on P B-R's yearly, end of school pilgrimages to visit his parents in Florida when it takes months to decide which novels to bring along, invariably ones he'd read in his 20's: last year's *The Red and the Black* a brilliant choice! (For next summer, he's vacillating mightily between *Sentimental Education* and the new translation of *Charterhouse of Parma*.)

In his brief pursuit of the labor theme, P B-R had considered rereading *Mary Barton*, the Elisabeth Gaskell novel about the Luddites, which he hardly remembers. First, he has to finish rereading the fabulous James novel, *The Tragic Muse*, about Miriam Rooth, the great, bohemian actress who entices many an uptight British aristocrat. He just got through the thrilling scene where Miriam is posing for her friend Nick, at his studio; after awhile, her whole self-consciously dramatic demeanor and diction suddenly shift into an utterly frank discussion of her life and career. Nick is a young, Liberal member of Parliament who, largely under Miriam's influence, will soon abandon his seat (along with his engagement to a wealthy and single-mindedly ambitious woman) to devote himself to portrait painting; the studio scene confirms the young pair's absolute egalitarian camaraderie as fellow artists. Last night, P B-R flashed back to the book's triumphant ending: this exotic Jewess marries the second rate actor she's been hanging out with the whole time, not taking any of the aristocrats' fervent proposals the least bit seriously.

P B-R does have some recent fiction by friends and colleagues at hand which he's been meaning to get to, right after the 19th century novels and assorted biographies (seeped in juicy anecdotes and delicious detail, à la Henry James). As for other contemporary fiction, he knows this sounds pretentious, but mostly it seems kind of beside the point after the magnificence of Proust, Kafka, Virginia Woolf and Beckett. Long ago, P B-R's own fictions had ineluctably veered into autobiography and screenplays, where they remain nestled among near essays and other gracious genres.

4.
MENTOR MOMENT/UM

Bayard Rustin became involved with his two significant mentors at almost the same time; benefiting from Rustin's expertise, each of these older men helped shape the slope of his career and ideological thinking, particularly in the crucible of the trio's shared commitment to Gandhian philosophy. On the day in June, 1941 that Rustin quit the Young Communist League, he walked from his Sugar Hill apartment (where he lived with his aunt and uncle, a schoolteacher and a chef in a midtown hotel) down to the "valley" of central Harlem to the headquarters of the Brotherhood of Sleeping Car Porters to renew a slight acquaintance of a few months with A. Philip Randolph, the leader of the nation's largest black union. A staunch anti-Communist and member of Norman Thomas' American Socialist Party, Randolph had already warned Bayard that Communists "are interested in utilizing civil rights for their own purposes."

Remaining his closest lifelong ally, Rustin was temporarily disillusioned shortly after beginning to help Randolph organize the upcoming mass civil rights march on Washington to protest the exclusion of black workers from defense industries, finally compelling Franklin D. Roosevelt to issue his executive order. Rustin was one of the younger militants conspiring to keep the march movement alive until the Armed Forces were desegregated—the same campaign he had been working on for the YCL. Randolph publicly categorized those individuals as "too enamored of the romantic flavor of demonstration…dilettantes or Communist dupes."

Rustin shifted to working with the predominantly white pacifist movement, specifically the Fellowship of Reconciliation—the American branch of an international movement of Christian pacifists, which was led by A.J. Muste, whom Randolph had also met several months earlier at an American Friends Service Committee conference. Muste was a former minister, and former member of a Trotskyite faction of the American labor movement. (In fact, it was on his return from visiting Trotsky in Switzerland that Muste stopped in Paris, where he underwent a conversion back to Christian pacifism.) Other early FOR members included Norman Thomas, then a Presbyterian minister in East Harlem, Rienhold Niebhur, rising theologian in New York, Howard Thurman, a professor of theology at Howard University, Rufus Jones and Henry Cadbury, Quaker intellectuals and founders of the American Friends Service Committee, and Oswald Garrison Villard, an editor of the *Nation* and grandson of the abolitionist William Lloyd Garrison.

At this time, Muste and A. Philip Randolph both belonged to a study group which met to discuss the applications of Gandhian philosophy to racial conditions in the U.S. For awhile, Rustin was head of the Free India Committee, and of course later became responsible for explicating Gandhi to Martin Luther King, Jr. Soon serving as the Fellowship's field secretary, Rustin traveled ten thousand miles through 20 states: organizing new pacifist groups, lecturing, teaching workshops in Gandhian techniques, visiting Civilian Public Service Work Camps where many of the conscientious objectors were interned during World War II, interceding on behalf of Japanese American families who were forcibly relocated after the bombing of Pearl Harbor. In the South, Rustin habitually challenged local Jim Crow laws in hotels and public transportation, resulting in frequent, severe beatings by police in and out of jail.

Rustin ended up spending 28 months in the penitentiary during WWII as a conscientious objector. Since he had been raised as a Quaker, in one of the few black Quaker families in eastern Pennsylvania, Rustin had the option of internment in a civilian work camp. (Toward the end of his life, he wrote that his activism "did not spring from being black. Rather, it is rooted fundamentally in my Quaker upbringing and the values instilled in me by the grandparents who raised me...based on the concept of a single human family and the belief that all members of that family are equal.") Rustin chose imprisonment, the alternative recommended by the more radical War Resisters League, but not the FOR, because work camps were created by the government and aided and abetted their conscription work. In the penitentiary, Rustin quickly became involved in hunger strikes and other protests over racially segregated accommodations and even prohibitions against interracial visiting among prisoners, for which he was often thrown into solitary confinement and exposed to beatings by white inmates. Fortunately, the Warden E.G. Hagerman held a Ph.D. and was related to the Brethren, which like the Religious Society of Friends, was one of America's historic peace churches. Although he wouldn't permit Rustin to teach American history, Hagerman did have him organizing a choir (which sang traditional Negro spirituals as well as medieval church music and Bach) and teaching dramatics (the inmates staged a memorable performance of Eugene O'Neill's *Emperor Jones*); Rustin also taught himself to play the lute in prison.

In 1948, Rustin began decades of international travel as peace emissary, as the American Friends Service Committee's delegate to an international peace conference in India. In 1952, FOR and the Friends collaborated to send Rustin to Africa to meet with leaders of the West African independence struggles, particularly Ghana's Kwame Nkrumah and Nigeria's Nhamdi Azikiwe, both of whom had once studied at Lincoln University in Pennsylvania. En route, Rustin visited Britain, also for the first time, where he attended an international meeting of Quakers, making a lasting impression on pacifists there. Years later, he helped plan the Aldermaston marches, protesting Britain's developing nuclear weaponry, which invigorated their peace movement, dormant since WWI; Rustin was the only American to speak at Trafalgar Square on a program featuring Bertrand Russell, Philip Toynbee and Doris Lessing.

Rustin's situation changed dramatically in 1953 when he was touring to raise money for a trip to Nigeria. Lecturing under the auspices of the American Association of University Women at the Pasadena Athletic

Club, he was approached by two audience members who invited him to join them at a nearby party. The next morning's issue of the *Los Angeles Times* reported that "Bayard Rustin, a 40-year-old nationally known Negro lecturer" was arrested on a "morals charge" when the police discovered him engaging in sexual acts with two young men in a parked car outside his hotel. Rustin was sentenced to 60 days in county jail, at which point A.J. Muste essentially abandoned him. Muste had been consistently advising Rustin to indulge his sexual preference in purely informal hours—not while undertaking an official mission for the FOR. (According to James Farmer, Muste had previously received a number of complaints from mothers around the country that "Bayard had led their sons astray.") Phoning Rustin on the west coast, Muste informed him that if he didn't resign as field secretary of the Fellowship, he would be fired.

Rustin had always been open about his sexuality, and generally supported by his family (especially his mother). When Bayard moved to Harlem in 1937, at age 25, he was quickly drawn to a well-respected elite society of homosexuals in the Sugar Hill area, largely centered around Hall Johnson, leader of the famous Hall Johnson Choir, and Alain Locke, an intellectual and professor at Howard University, educated at Harvard and the University of Berlin, as was W.E.B. DuBois. Writing from jail to John Swomley, Muste's chief assistant, for the first time Rustin took a sadly repentant attitude (à la Oscar Wilde) about his sexuality:

> But I know that, in God's way of turning ugliness and personal defeat to triumph, I have gone deeper in the past six weeks than ever before, and I feel that I have at last seen the real problem. It has been pride—self.
>
> I know now that for me sex must be sublimated, if I am to live with myself and in this world longer. For it would be better to be dead than to do worse than those I have denounced from the platform as murderers. Violence is not as bad as violence *and* hypocrisy...

Not long after leaving the Fellowship, Rustin complained that A.J. Muste had cut him off, penniless. He did receive several checks from the

FOR, but after twelve years of service, Rustin felt entitled to substantial severance pay. Muste had also encouraged Rustin to seek a cure in psychotherapy, stating the FOR would pay if Rustin himself was unable to do so. However, Muste soon withdrew that offer, at a time when Rustin was scrambling for money, doing menial work and repairing people's harpsichords and musical instruments. To continue treatment, his psychoanalyst had to pull strings to get Rustin into a clinic at Roosevelt Hospital. "Dr. A" reports: "At the beginning, his warm feeling for A.J. Muste was a centerpiece of the therapeutic sessions we had. He wanted very much to present Muste as a kind and fatherly man. But as we continued working together…I helped him to recognize that Muste wasn't quite the saint that he, Rustin, wanted to see—that in the end, Muste didn't really give a damn about him."

It was the more secular War Resisters League that rescued Rustin from what had looked like political oblivion. When the sex scandal hit, Rustin offered to withdraw from their advisory council. Instead, they asked him to become executive secretary, a position which Rustin held for 12 years, strengthening ties between the pacifist and civil rights movements, and acting as roving troubleshooter, particularly in Africa. A.J. Muste abruptly ended his association with the WRL; reconsidering, he resumed working with the group and with Bayard, but without any of the personal warmth that had formerly marked their relationship. Rustin was also deeply hurt by the coolness of the American Friends Service Committee, which persisted after his rehabilitation with the WRL. Within two years, Rustin was immersed in the Montgomery bus boycott, partly on the insistence of its chief leader, E.D. Nixon, a veteran organizer with the Brotherhood of Sleeping Car Porters. Close collaboration with Randolph led to Rustin becoming director of the A. Philip Randolph Institute when it was founded in 1965, to cement the alliance of labor and civil rights advocacy.

Rustin and Randolph had a great deal in common temperamentally and even physically as well as ideologically. Both were tall, strikingly handsome, elegantly dressed, with impeccable manners and a kind of inviolable dignity. C.L. Dellums, Randolph's friend since 1926 and an organizer of the Oakland chapter of the Brotherhood, said, "That man had so much dignity, it was as much a part of him as his limbs." Jervis Anderson also wrote a compelling biography of A. Philip Randolph in which he relates an incident at the historic civil rights march from Selma to Montgomery, where Randolph and Rustin had flown with one hundred others for the final day. At the Montgomery airport, Randolph suffered one of his spells of dizziness from a heart ailment, and collapsed. "I've never seen anything like that," reported Rochelle Horowitz, Rustin's collaborator and secretary. "No one ever fell backwards like that. His eyes were wide open, and he was still bolt upright—going down with absolute dignity." Rustin held off photographers with his fists. "He said nobody was going to get a shot of Randolph flat on his back."

Both Randolph and Rustin were self-styled, and both had cultivated accents that puzzled their fellow African Americans as well as more than a few whites. Rustin was a modern Anglophile, favoring the crisp diction and accent of the British upper class. Randolph spoke in a grave cadence, which he probably thought of as that of the great, New England abolitionist preachers and speakers of the nineteenth century, though there was also an old southern gravitas in his style of delivery. (His father had been the pastor of an American Methodist Episcopal church in Jacksonville, Florida, and Rustin's maternal grandfather was deacon of an AME church in Pennsylvania.) Reportedly, Randolph's speeches were so eloquent that many members of the labor council assumed he was Harvard educated, therefore out of touch with working people. (Actually, like Rustin, Randolph had attended City College evenings without graduating, where he too had been an activist, with the socialist movement of Eugene Debs.) As young men, both had some voice training: Randolph was a Shakespearean actor in Florida, and Rustin sang gospel; early on in New York, he did a stint in a Broadway musical starring Paul Robeson, and Rustin also supported himself briefly by singing with Josh White and Leadbelly in the Village.

In the closing years of his life, Rustin was to be Randolph's most solicitous friend and guardian. In May, 1969, soon after his 80th birthday, Randolph was honored at a black tie dinner in the Grand Ballroom of the Waldorf Astoria, with more than 1200 people present on the ballroom floor and another 80—each a birthday "candle"—on the dais; Randolph's old friends Eubie Blake and Noble Sissle led the six-piece band. (In the 1920s, Sissle, a young vocalist and lyricist and his partner Blake, the pianist and composer, had enjoyed great success on Broadway with the hit musical, *Shuffle Along*.) At the party, Rustin declared that with the exception of his grandparents, "no one had stood beside me in times of trial the way Mr. Randolph has. He is the only man I know who has never said an unkind word about anyone, or who refuses to listen to an unkind word about anyone, even though it may be true."

Several years later, Rustin moved the widowed and childless Randolph out of Harlem and next door to him in the International Ladies Garment Workers Union building in the Chelsea district downtown. Not long before Randolph died in 1979, at the age of 90, Arnold Aronson, of the Leadership Conference on Civil Rights, joined both men at dinner. "It was a moving thing to see," Aronson remembered. "Bayard was encouraging Randolph to eat, as if Randolph was the child and Bayard the parent. Bayard would cut the meat and feed Randolph bits of it, with such tenderness and caring. It reinforced my old feeling that Randolph was the father Bayard never had, and that Bayard was the son Randolph never had."

5.
"BEYOND CATEGORY":
BILLY STRAYHORN AND THE DUKE

The cold and brilliant (light) light is again flooding through the window. The glowing sky can be seen outside exactly as the tattered and bohemian prophets predicted long ago. The varied play of light seems to come not only from the window but from all sides: through the walls and the cracks in the cupboard, from the furniture. The unearthly producer, the set-designer, and the lighting specialist would do well to remember that the birth of any extraordinary human being most definitely suggests the mingled presence of terror and dignified beauty.

BILLY STRAYHORN was Duke Ellington's arranger for nearly 3 decades. Strayhorn composed the Ellington Orchestra's theme song, and greatest success, "Take the A Train," and was co-composer of "Satin Doll" and many other jazz standards introduced by the orchestra. Their working relationship was unique, "beyond category," as Ellington liked to say about his own music; on stage, Ellington usually referred to Strayhorn with cryptic aesthetic intimacy as "our writing and arranging companion," and the media typically tagged him as Duke's alter ego. (Ellington commented, "Let's not go overboard. Swee' Pea is only my right arm, left foot, eyes, stomach, ears, and soul not my ego.") Strayhorn was on the payroll until he died at age 51: on call for consultation (frequently via long distance phone calls in the middle of the night), he might be sent anywhere in the country to work on just about any type of project, from intensive sessions with a young Lena Horne (who considered Strayhorn "my other self" and with whom Ellington was having a secret affair) to orchestrating a play for Orson Welles. It has become evident that Strayhorn composed far more music than the listening public knows—hit songs, concert works, film scores, music for a Broadway show. Often, Strayhorn's name didn't appear on the final copyrighted materials, even of songs which he had written entirely himself.

From the time 23-year-old Billy Strayhorn, a brilliant and self-styled pianist and urbane songwriter in the Gershwin/Cole Porter mode, came to New York in 1939 at Ellington's behest, virtually all of his works were recorded by Ellington or members of his orchestra. These were published by several companies in a manner fairly typical for the era—that is, through a knotty mesh of conflicting strategies difficult to entangle from the outside. It was axiomatic that the composer would not necessarily be the immediate or chief beneficiary of his own work (and arrangers were seldom credited). In fact, Ellington himself had been an historic victim of this system several years earlier, when he was under contract to Irving Mills: the publishing mogul took credit for co-composing or writing lyrics for more than fifty Ellington works, including such masterpieces as "In a Sentimental Mood," "Mood Indigo," "Prelude in a Kiss," "Solitude," and "Sophisticated Lady." Fortunately for Ellington, no one really believed that Mills wrote anything. But some of Strayhorn's publishing problems were unique: compositions correctly credited to him on record labels were not copyrighted in his name; other songs were recorded and issued with the proper composer credit, then not copyrighted at all; some solitary contributions as well as collaborations were credited solely to Ellington. Since most of these works were published by Ellington's own company, Tempo Music, Strayhorn's publishing problems were primarily with Ellington.

Customarily self-effacing in regard to public recognition yet confident that he enjoyed the unqualified respect of fellow musicians and jazz aficionados, sometimes Strayhorn did try to establish a more independent artistic career. In the early 1950s, he looked into his royalty situation. "That was the first time I saw any conflict between the old man and Strayhorn," his son Mercer Ellington remembered. "They had a talk about it, but Strayhorn wasn't satisfied, and he pulled away. There was some distance between them." In the handful of interviews published or broadcasted during his career, Strayhorn refrained from noting this rift. For one thing, Ellington had given him stock (ten shares) in Tempo Music when the company was formed in 1941, and through it Strayhorn had been profiting from all of their published compositions. In addition, Ellington's financial generosity toward Strayhorn was legendary: rent and living expenses, his vast and lavish wardrobe, the finest food and drink, travel—anything Strayhorn seemed to need or want was his.

"Money wasn't quite the problem. How could it be when Billy had everything?" commented jazz critic and producer Leonard Feather. "The problem was the lack of independence that his business problems represented...The actual source of his frustration was artistic." Unique in jazz history for sustaining a musical organization for decades, one way Duke Ellington engendered loyalty was through liberation: he kept his cats at home by letting them loose to do their own projects. About this time, his star saxophone soloist, Johnny Hodges, was grumbling about leaving. Ellington arranged for Hodges to make his own records by reviving the dormant small-band phase of his operation and launching a new label, Mercer Records, jointly owned by him, Leonard Feather and the company's namesake. Strayhorn's creative role was to serve as musical director and arranger as well as pianist on many of the label's dates, and he would be given full credit for every aspect of his participation. However, they were producing 78 rpm's, while record buyers were shifting to 33 1/3 LPS, and Mercer Records folded in ten months.

After 14 years of dueting with Ellington, theater became the fulcrum of Strayhorn's reemergence. He began by working on the score for a summer stock version of *Cabin in the Sky* that was being put together by Herbert Machiz, a colleague home from Paris. In February, 1953, Machiz founded the Artists' Theater in New York, which in its first year presented, among others, new plays by Tennessee Williams, Frank O'Hara, John Ashbery and James Merrill with sets by Larry Rivers, Elaine de Kooning and Grace Hartigan. Strayhorn contributed to the off-Broadway theater's only play with music, a dramatic musical adaptation of Federico Garcia Lorca's tragic lament to doomed romance, "The Love of Don Perlimin for Belisa in Their Garden," performed by an all black cast. Then he set out to write a musical incorporating elements of jazz, with Julliard-trained Luther Henderson: Ellington sabotaged this effort by confiding to each one separately that the other would seriously cramp his style. In 1955, Strayhorn accompanied Lena Horne on piano for fourteen recordings made by RCA, and supervised by her husband, Lenny Hayton; Strayhorn was also indulging his passion which had lain dormant since his early career, for writing love song lyrics.

When Strayhorn returned from visiting Paris, Ellington initiated a new level of collaboration, offering to share composing credits; moreover, he encouraged Strayhorn to come up with original concepts, not to merely execute Ellington's ideas. (Any changes in their financial arrangements are impossible to trace since many of Strayhorn's bills were paid directly by Ellington's organization, in part with Ellington's personal funds.) Ellington's reputation was on the upswing, mainly due to the sensation he had created at the 3rd Newport Jazz Festival: in the middle of "Diminuendo and Crescendo in Blue," Ellington added a mammoth "wailing interval," a fifteen-minute, twenty-seven chorus uninterrupted solo blues improvisation by tenor saxophonist Paul Gonsalves, a be-bop oriented veteran of Dizzy Gillespie's band (while Ellington egged him on, revving his arms like a drivetrain). In the mid '50s, the collaborators branched out into an impressive array of new modes and projects, which continued for the rest of Strayhorn's career: their Shakespearean suite, "Such Sweet Thunder," premiered at Manhattan's Town Hall before going onto the venue which had commissioned it, the Stratford Music Festival, an offshoot of the Shakespearean Festival in Stratford, Ontario, founded in 1953 by the English director, Sir Tyrone Guthrie.

Credited as collaborator on "Such Sweet Thunder," Strayhorn immediately went to work on a CBS special, "A Drum Is a Woman," for the U.S. Steel Hour, then plunged into a series of new arrangements for "Ella Fitzgerald Sings the Duke Ellington Songbook" (frustrated that she and Ellington were too busy touring to confer in person, Ella Fitzgerald almost canceled the project). Ellington was true to his word, but his publicist Joe Morgen had an intense, homophobic hatred of Strayhorn and systematically eliminated any mention of his name from the major publicity Morgen was getting for Ellington in *Newsweek*, *Look* and the *New York Times*. Mercer Ellington (who wasn't raised by Duke, and who seemed to feel an ambivalent, sibling rivalry toward Strayhorn) commented, "Pop ran his business like a family, and his family like a business…Your sons, you let them fend for themselves—that's how they learn and how they get stronger…You pit one against the other, really. That's the way the old man functioned as far as people like Joe Morgen and Strayhorn and myself were concerned. You let them fight it out." He added that Duke had a more protective attitude toward daughters, which was more typically how he treated Strayhorn.

Honi Coles (an originator of the Copasetics, Strayhorn called Coles "Father" and even sent him Father's Day cards) remembers a dinner conversation right after the *Newsweek* article appeared. Strayhorn rarely complained about his professional reputation or any aspect of his complex relationship with Ellington, and Coles was trying to push him to admit his feelings. At first Strayhorn responded, "'Oh, Father, you know about these things. I don't care.'" When Coles said, "'I think you do care or you wouldn't be drinking like a fucking fish every fucking time I see you,'" Strayhorn broke down crying. However, Coles understood why Strayhorn insisted he was better off that way: "Because he wasn't a celebrity, he didn't have to answer to anybody about his lifestyle." A friend, and fellow gay black musician, declared that Strayhorn was the only musician he knew in the 1940s who "had the strength to make an extraordinary decision…not to hide the fact that he was homosexual." Famously egalitarian, Ellington's support was crucial in allowing Strayhorn to do that: by providing acceptance which he had never received from his father, by offering a high profile outlet for his artistry, and mostly by permanently putting Strayhorn on payroll, freeing him from the hardships he would have faced in seeking a career as a pianist or bandleader.

In the 1960s Ellington flourished, signing up for jazz festivals which were sprouting all over the country in Newport's image. Somewhat detached and drinking even more heavily than usual, Strayhorn did become intensely engaged in a collaborative adaptation of Tchaikovsky's *Nutcracker Suite* ballet for jazz orchestra, which entailed a great deal of discussion, closely listening to the original composition, and many long distance phone consultations. They collaborated on scores for Otto Preminger's *Anatomy of a Murder*, and for *Paris Blues*, about American jazz musicians living in Paris, starring Sidney Poitier and Paul Newman, with Joanne Woodward and Diahann Carrol as the love interests. (Diahann Carroll called Billy a "beautiful, delicate little flower...a tortured genius." She said, "I got exactly the same feeling being in the presence of James Baldwin...both knew the cruelness of the world, and that's what I thought was part of the enormous sadness beneath their exteriors.") Duke Ellington's new contract gave him control of producing LPs, and he put out several albums of Strayhorn classics. On the other hand, when Frank Sinatra started his own label, Reprise, and wanted Strayhorn to come work with him, Ellington prevented it: "'When Duke found out, he blew his fuckin' top,'" reported Al Hibbler, former Ellington vocalist then with Sinatra.

The first extended period that Strayhorn had worked independently of Ellington occurred a decade earlier, in the 1940s, due to wholly unforeseen circumstances. In 1941, a prolonged legal battle between the American Society of Composers, Authors and Publishers (ASCAP) and the radio industry came to an unexpected head: radio stations were refusing to submit to an ASCAP-produced increase in fees that gave stations the right to broadcast music by ASCAP members. Launching their own organization, called Broadcast Music Inc. (BMI), the stations announced they would not air any music by ASCAP members. This was tantamount to a ban on popular music, including almost all the best known works of Ellington who had been a member since 1935. In order to perform on radio, Ellington needed practically a whole new repertoire, which he himself couldn't write or even co-write.

Billy Strayhorn had never joined ASCAP, nor had Mercer Ellington who hadn't composed much music yet. "Strayhorn and I got this big break at the same time," remembered Mercer. "Overnight, literally we got the chance to write a whole new book for the band. It could have taken us twenty years to get the old man to make room for that much of our music." The duo holed up in a Chicago hotel working day and night, sleeping in shifts, fueled by a gallon jug of blackberry wine. Strayhorn produced a stack of songs, including "After All," "Clementine," "Johnny Come Lately," "A Flower Is a Lovesome Thing," and "Take the A Train" (which Mercer rescued from the garbage: Strayhorn had considered it too derivative of Fletcher Henderson, Benny Goodman's arranger and a key to his rise as King of Swing).

Strayhorn's most ambitious piece was "Chelsea Bridge," an impressionistic miniature composed, he said, with a painting by James McNeill Whistler in mind. Unlike conventional tune-based pop and jazz numbers of the day, "Chelsea Bridge" is classical in its integration of melody and harmony as an organic whole. There is more Debussy than Ellington in "Chelsea Bridge," though Ellington himself, trained as a painter, had long been experimenting with imaginatively colored tone poems. Comparably sophisticated, but much different in style, "Johnny Come Lately" was a proto-bop piece which emerged from the hipster experimentation of Strayhorn's after hour sessions with Dizzy Gillespie and Max Roach. Ellington described Strayhorn's new arrangement of "Flamingo" as the "renaissance of vocal orchestration." Pianist and composer John Lewis commented that it "had nothing to do with what had gone on in jazz at all before. It sounded as if Stravinsky were a jazz musician."

Both classically trained pianists, virtually everything about Billy Strayhorn and Duke Ellington made them a good match. When first introduced in Pittsburgh by a mutual friend, George Greenlee, Duke immediately requested, "'Sit down at the piano, and let me hear what you can do.'" Strayhorn responded, "'Mr. Ellington, this is the way you played this number in the show,'" and according to Greenlee, "Billy played it *exactly* like Duke." "'Now this is the way *I* would play it.'" Changing keys and upping the tempo slightly, Strayhorn shifted into an adaptation which Greenlee described as "pretty hip sounding and further and further 'out there' as he went on." From the outset, Strayhorn had no job description, contract, or even a verbal understanding of his responsibilities or terms of compensation. The arrangement was as much familial as it was professional: Ellington would take care of Billy. In fact, when he moved to New York, Strayhorn stayed at the YMCA only one night; he came to visit Ellington's sister, Ruth, his lover Mildred Dixon and Mercer at their posh Sugar Hill apartment, and moved right in (Ellington also lived there when he wasn't touring). Ruth Ellington commented, "We all loved Billums like he was our very own. Edward arranged it that way, and we thought that whatever he did was wonderful. That's the way we were trained."

Ellington represented the urbane sophistication which Strayhorn had been longing for in his own life. As a young man yearning to leave Pittsburgh, he avidly read the *New Yorker*; Ellington *was* one, as Strayhorn could become by working with him. While Strayhorn hoped to emulate Stravinsky, Duke Ellington was already being seen in some informed circles as the modernist's peer; as early as 1933, discerning critics were recognizing in him a black composer comparable to Ravel and Stravinsky. In addition, Ellington projected an air of continental polish: stately to the verge of ostentation, Ellington used vast resources of ingenuity and will to project an image that promoted pride in and respect for black identity. Yet the priorities of a traveling bandleader—and one who was a tireless composer, arranger, record producer and entrepreneur as well—prevented Ellington from diving into the high culture he strove to embody. By contrast, Strayhorn studied the music scores of the masters, and immersed himself in New York's museums and cultural life (frequently exploring with Lena Horne who thought of him as her guru). When Ellington was asked to compose a Shakespearean suite, it was evident he had never read Shakespeare, and would rely heavily on Strayhorn, whose loving expertise had been well established on the band bus, where he sometimes got into debates about the Bard with the more literate band members. ("We used to *call* him Shakespeare—that was one of his nicknames," said Jimmy Hamilton.)

Strayhorn's chief independent artistic existence involved a circle of black and mostly gay creative people in New York, who met informally in the late 1940s. The Neal Salon, as it came to be called, was founded by Frank Neal, a dancer (formerly with Katherine Dunham) and painter trained at the Chicago Art Institute, and his wife Dorcas. Regulars included dancer and choreographer, Tally Beatty, painter and playwright

Charles Sebree, the actor and singer Brock Peters, Harry Belafonte, the painter Felrath Hines; Eartha Kitt and John Cage also dropped in occasionally, as did James Baldwin when he was in the city (he and Strayhorn were habitués and stars of the Mars Club in Paris, an internationally known gay spot where Strayhorn's longtime companion Aaron Bridgers was house pianist). Gathering around midnight, the group would talk all night. Dorcas Neal characterized the Neal Salon as a family, comparing them to Bloomsbury. "They all faced a lot of the same problems regarding their careers and their place in the world, which was white at the time. I think they were able to answer many of those questions for each other and solve those problems and become successful in the world."

Early in 1950, Strayhorn accepted an invitation to become a member of a more formal organization, a society of black tap dancers called the Copasetics, founded in honor of tap icon Bill "Bojangles" Robinson who was credited with coining the term to express soft-shoe felicity. The idea for the group came from several dancers while waiting in line in the pitiless cold outside the Harlem Armory where Robinson's wake was being held. Strayhorn was elected president and his apartment soon became their clubhouse. The Copasetics had already sponsored a dance at Big George's Barbecue in Queens, the highlight of which was an impromptu performance on bass fiddle by the prizefighter Ezzard Charles. Strayhorn decided they would stage an annual, original musical revue. A typical skit: the Copasetics, portraying policemen, barge into a garage to bust some crap-shooting hoodlums and their dames, but the game beckons and the cops play, joining the gamblers and their ladies for a production number.

In 1957, more than eleven hundred ticket buyers—almost all show-business insiders and figures in black society—paid fifteen dollars apiece to attend the Copasetics Cruise held at the Riviera Terrace Room, a swank banquet hall on West 73rd Street. "Anybody who was anybody had to be there," said Rachel Robinson, the wife of Jackie Robinson. The couple attended nearly every year; in 1957, they were in the company of Lena Horne and Lenny Hayton, Miles Davis, Willie Mays and others. "People waited all year for the next Copasetics night," added Robinson.

Although it was of great importance to the community, it was never acknowledged, even in a passing reference, in a single New York publication beyond the black press. Duke Ellington supported the organization by advertising Tempo Music in the souvenir booklets, but he never attended any Copasetics events. "I believe he didn't want to upstage Billy," commented Honi Coles. "I give him credit for that."

6.
SWEET, SAUCY SUMMER

Now that summer is here—more than just here, but breezing by at a lovely yet alarmingly brisk clip—predictably, Peripatetic Book-Reviewer finds himself torn among writing, traveling, reading (fewer novels since school ended, he must be feeling less need to escape), snoozing, hanging out with friends at the beach (rather, taking late afternoon walks when the sun isn't too strong) or at the nighttime zoo (San Diego's finest moment). Truthfully, P B-R had already ruled out traveling as too expensive: lucky to be getting José's apartment in LA for a week in August, when they'll be in Italy (though P B-R had been prepared to spring for a hotel). For the life of him, he can't figure out how he ever afforded taking Mr. Mister to Vancouver that summer, not to mention the New York hotels—except that San Diego rents were so much cheaper then.

Also predictably, only the least compelling of P B-R's several writing projects involves any compensation. The one he hasn't started yet: doing follow-up phone interviews, and summary write ups, with grant recipients of a federal program to deal with community violence. Anyway, P B-R has nearly finished the piece on the (un)changing faces of poverty, which he took on mostly for the opportunity to finally read the much-vaunted (and rightly so) Isserman biography of Michael Harrington. His friend Ernie is putting together a poverty reader, possibly for South End Press: a resumé item for P B-R, potentially leading to further unremunerative essays.

Somehow, he had managed to remain largely unaware of all the political machinations of the old, non-Marxist left confronting the New Left over Vietnam, despite being very active in the anti-war movement (spending numerous years in constant meetings). Today, Harrington's tactics (for which he repeatedly apologized, doing some successful damage control) just sound so dumb and heavy-handed, entirely unworthy of a former, stalwart Catholic Worker—like censoring SDS mailings and locking out student leaders (who quickly broke the locks then confiscated the mailing lists). Especially stupid, since as Isserman cogently points out, in essence SDS was in agreement with SLID, the Socialist group that sponsored the Port Huron conference, about the value of "participatory democracy" over communism: only they couldn't see the Soviet Union as the same magnitude of threat insisted upon by the Socialists. P B-R had always been grateful that there really wasn't much sectarianism involved in San Diego coalition building besides the occasional Stalinist hoping to liquidate a random Trot in the Socialist Workers Party (the east coast was much worse, presumably LA too). Or periodically, the SWP or any of the multitude of small Maoist parties would pack a meeting, trying to force a vote on one of their high priority issues (at least SWP members had the courtesy to identify themselves as such).

Practically everybody P B-R was close to then was some shade of independent leftist, for whom "imperialism" was the ultimate dirty word. They all tended to be wary of Marxist-Leninists who were so totally outside the counter-culture: with their bizarrely Catholic, or puritanical dictum of sex serving to make babies for the revolution; required to tow absurdly unrealistic party lines (a friend formerly on the central committee of the Maoist PLP related how they would be ordered to call for a strike in situations where zero groundwork had been laid). And their cardinal sins: unlike Trotskyites, Marxists-Leninists were wholly disinterested in feminism, and ridiculously homophobic, insisting that class was the primary contradiction. (P B-R agreed, which didn't suggest it was the only important concern, or even necessarily the best organizing principle.) After a decade of gay liberation and the "lavender left," they were still promulgating the "bourgeois decadence" line: an unfortunate bi-product of capitalism, homosexuals would simply wither away one fine day, along with the too too solid state itself.

One of P B-R's favorite stories used to concern a household of lesbian members of the Maoist Communist Workers Party, where P B-R would sometimes hang out with his friend Toni: like all of them, an ex-grad student who had joined the workers at a local shipbuilding factory. (A few had jobs in power plants, so when the call came, they could shut them down!—always striking P B-R as the very epitome of delusion.) He would watch them getting into remarkably unsuitable drag to go to their cell meeting: flannel shirts and work boots yielded to nylons and skirts, complete with make-up and slightly teased hair. Suddenly, in the early '80s, the CWP newspaper boldly announced that gays and lesbians are oppressed people too, therefore they must be assumed to possess revolutionary potential! The article was written by one of these women, under the hilarious pseudonym, Mara Maath: the CWP sent her to the east coast on a national gay and lesbian recruiting tour (apparently taking their oppression wherever they could find it). P B-R never did discover what "Mara" wore there.

In retrospect, it remains bewildering that the non-Marxist left seemed to have spent more energy on fighting Marxists rather than the supporters of the Vietnam War. P B-R does understand how acutely aware Socialists must have been that their power had peaked long ago with Eugene Debs; probably, they needed to resort to a variety of illusions to maintain optimism. Nevertheless, it had been awhile since those parties had any real drawing power: 1956 was when Khrushchev characterized Stalin publicly as a bloody, paranoid tyrant. P B-R remembers the moving chapter in Dorothy Healey's autobiography (written with Isserman too) which he's taught several times in personal narrative writing classes, describing the big meeting in New York where that historic speech was first revealed to the CPUSA; previously they'd only been hearing vaguely ominous references to Stalin's "cult of personality." A devastated Healey (until then, resolutely discounting anti-Stalinism as capitalist propaganda) still didn't quit the party for many more years. However, Communist Party membership, already at a low point due to McCarthyism, was further decimated.

Most enigmatic is how any Socialist could have believed that their best shot lay with Johnson and the poverty program: a marker for P B-R of a huge generation gap. He can vaguely imagine it with someone like Rustin, who had helped accomplish something major, in terms of legislative changes: maybe they began to identify with success itself, to convince themselves the establishment was mutable, at least neutral, or not structurally malevolent as Harrington himself (who was regularly conferring at the White House for a brief period) had suggested in *The Other America*. Honestly, though, how could anyone on the left have placed one iota of trust in Johnson (or in JFK, for that matter)? P B-R had never paid much attention to electoral politics, but he remembers the most vilified characters at Brandeis were precisely those former leftist professors working in the Johnson administration. Paul, a poli sci major and red diaper baby, had entertained a special loathing for John Roche, whose name keeps popping up lately in P B-R's readings, as a chief Harrington/Rustin ally.

P B-R's most vivid memory of that kind has to do with the school board fights in Brownsville, the section of Brooklyn where his parents grew up, and where he visited his grandmother (who refused to move away, to his parents' dismay) until her death in 1961. P B-R will never forget the shrieking banner headlines of the *Guardian*—"ANKER, SHANKER and the BANKERS!"—because Debby Anker was a good friend at Brandeis (and Kathy Acker's roommate, so P B-R was privy to Kathy gossip, though he scarcely knew her then). (Coming from a thoroughly mercantile family in Yonkers, as a freshman P B-R had been amazed at how many parents were famous media figures, artists, or at least professors.) Debby was mortified by the idea that her father, head of the New York City Board of Education, was in collusion against "the people," or against community control, which at the time seemed such a bottom-line, sacrosanct principle, despite frequently discussed contradictions: most communities were full of rednecks, and it was actually the federal government and judiciary which had been mandating desegregation.

In college, P B-R didn't go to meetings, but he participated in many civil rights sit-ins and anti-war demonstrations (which grew from several hundred beleaguered protestors his freshman year to many thousands by the time he graduated). His first, classic sit-in was at Boston's federal building when Johnson wouldn't send troops to Selma. By far the most romantic one was a weekend in front of the White House which Huntley-Brinkley termed a "slush-in" (it was snowing and they were under plastic tarps). On the chartered bus back to school, P B-R maneuvered to sit next to Nick, whom he'd had a raging crush on all freshman year. As virtually the only blond at Brandeis, Nick was the object of nearly universal lust: being bisexual, and prodigiously endowed, he diligently fulfilled his destiny until handily flunking out of school. P B-R lied: he had dreamt about sitting next to Nick on this bus ride, he murmured, as they groped each other under the blanket. Some time later, P B-R threw up out the window (luckily, the bus wasn't moving)—he hadn't eaten much, and wasn't used to coffee or physical contact. Then they had sex in Nick's dorm room, while Richard agitatedly knocked on the door (pursuing them both with variable success, Richard had anxiously been awaiting the bus's return). P B-R found this long-anticipated, first time with a man just as confusing as his futile attempts with women but vastly more exciting.

From the outset, P B-R's political activities were calculated: in high school, he attended CORE meetings in downtown Yonkers; he grew a beard the summer before freshman year, and started tutoring in Roxbury his first semester. Strongly influenced by existentialism in high school and beginning what would stretch into almost a decade of therapy, P B-R reasoned: he was unable to like himself, he realized, mostly due to guilt about his sexuality, and suppressed-rage-turned-into-depression about being made to feel that guilt. But by his actions, primarily political ones, at least P B-R could come to respect himself. In college, that line of thought also led to working for Operation Headstart, then intensively in the mental hospital.

Although in San Diego in the '70s he was heavily involved with downtown artists' coalitions and a farmworkers' support group, that seems a very long time ago. Now all P B-R wants to do (aside from having sex, of course) is read, write and hang out with friends.

He really must find a way to get back east next summer. He's never laid eyes on Debby's adopted son, met Paul's wife and her kids once, and for that matter, has only seen his own nephew the one time he and Mr. were in the Hamptons with them, before Dave's divorce. (Probably P B-R wouldn't contact his other brother, who seems to relish every opportunity to break dates, and insult him.) Bett had gone through the whole regimen of chemo and radiation since he was last in Baltimore. However, this sedentary, or stationary summer has been excellent for writing, and for hanging out with old friends he rarely sees during school. Partly relaxed because next year's teaching is set, momentarily P B-R doesn't need to think about income, moving or classes (he's taught them all before)—regular, intense sex with semi-hustler, semi-boyfriend Marcus hasn't been hurting either. (As a "tweeker" who's breaking parole, though, Marcus is likely to vanish at any moment: being black, he'll end up in jail, not rehab, Prop. 36 notwithstanding.)

Is P B-R losing some of his wanderlust, or perhaps the need to view himself in those terms? Could he possibly be liking San Diego better lately? He *has* been meeting exceptional new people (which usually seems extremely improbable) like Susan, a lesbian Russian film scholar, and some of her 40ish gay, academic friends. Still maintaining that he hates condos, he's considering trying to buy one, while dubious about qualifying for a loan because his yearly income can be so variable. But P B-R has been telling himself that it's his only option, since San Diego rents are skyrocketing. He's afraid of being forced out of Hillcrest, his gay walking neighborhood (infamous briefly à la Andrew Cunanan), with restaurants, Landmark movie theaters and convenient shuttle to campus. In the past, it had been easy enough to rent a decent-sized, inexpensive apartment, and sublet it to a student for a semester or two when P B-R left town, plus put money aside into mutual funds (a potential future down payment): those days are definitely over.

When he goes to Florida again in September, he'll consult his mother about help, also pretending to ask his father whose attention span is brief. P B-R doesn't expect much: his mother is generous, and admirably without guilt trips; but she's unrealistic about the cost of living. Besides, she has consistently maintained that one buys real estate solely to raise a family. P B-R was never sure to what extent she was punishing him for not producing kids. In any case, Dave will be in Florida too: P B-R's strongest partisan, in favored position as youngest, highly successful, child. Having already visited his parents once this summer, P B-R felt that he needed to get back there again, which was unlikely after school started: his father is too out of it for them to travel to New York anymore to see family, including several beloved nieces and nephews (P B-R is hoping they'll make more frequent trips to Florida), and to just generally be around people not all in their 80's, dying and with Alzheimer's.

True, the last time P B-R had to move, he repeatedly thanked his lucky stars he was renting, and not trapped next door to that psychotic gay couple (crystal freaks, despite the daddy being retired military). The final straw came when P B-R overheard them on their balcony, which was draped in a gigantic rainbow flag, emblem of aggressive pride, harassing a harmless, slightly disabled woman picking flowers at the union hall next door. Within minutes, they were threatening, "we know where you live, and we're going to get you"; in turn, she assured them she had a gun (as P B-R instantly imagined her missing their window and hitting his own). Piqued that she couldn't decipher his speech impediment, the 40-something, perpetually shirtless "boy" (who soon rushed down to the street to physically confront this brazen flower thief) screeched, "What, are you deaf, BITCH?" When she replied that, actually, the doctor *had* said the cancer left her hearing impaired, he retorted in an insane yelp, "WHAT? YOU THINK I GIVE A FUCK ABOUT YOUR CANCER, BITCH?!"

P B-R vividly documented this and other incidents in a letter headed "Clear and Present Danger" (and in his mind, "Only In San Diego") to his loathsome landlady (whom he'd always found a repulsive combination of slothful and self-righteous), such as the gruesome duo dumping garbage on the downstairs neighbor's doorstep as well as accusing all of his own black visitors of stealing their bicycle which, ignoring P B-R's warning, they had left outside overnight, unlocked. Though he rapidly found a very desirable place to move with an incredible canyon view, weeding through closets, endless file cabinets, and packing way too many books took up most of the past summer. So P B-R is determined to continue enjoying this one in his bright and breezy (and expensive) apartment.

7.
HIGH AND LOW

Bayard Rustin and Billy Strayhorn, both very socially active, ran in overlapping artistic, and (in sometimes feuding) political circles. In particular, both were quite close to Arthur and Marian Logan whose brownstone on West 88th Street became a center for New York's black elite, like Rachel and Jackie Robinson, Lena Horne, Harry Belafonte, and Sarah Vaughan. Arthur Logan was friend and personal physician to Martin Luther King, Jr., Rustin, Duke Ellington, Strayhorn and many of their acquaintances, including most of the Copasetics, who were all among the Logans' frequent house guests. (A chronic hypochondriac, Ellington would call Logan at 4 or 5 a.m., according to Marian, "just to make sure that Arthur would pick up the phone in case he might really need him for something.")

Deeply involved in charitable and civil rights work, in the mid '60s, Arthur was active in New York's hospital system and head of the city's poverty programs, while Marian was on the board of SCLC. Strayhorn often helped the Logans organize fundraisers for SCLC with a hundred or so of their most affluent friends: typically, Martin Luther King, Jr. would give a short, inspirational speech and Strayhorn played, "Why Don't You Do Right" on the piano (its chorus, which he didn't sing, ends with the lyric, "Get out of here and get me some money too").

The Logans were elegant, personable and cultured. He was over six feet, with green eyes, light skin, delicate features, and he wore a thin moustache. ("I got used to the dirty looks from people who thought I was hanging on a white man and a doctor, yet," said Marian.) Arthur's father, Warren Logan, had been on the faculty of Tuskegee Institute, and

Arthur was born on campus. Moving to New York at age 10, he attended the famous, racially integrated Ethical Culture School, graduated Phi Beta Kappa from Williams College, and went on to medical school at Columbia University. His wife, Marian Bruce, had sung in supper clubs, and it was probably through her that Logan met Ellington. Since their marriage in 1958, she had largely ceded her musical career to a role as one of black society's grand hostesses. Very self-possessed, Marian "wore her good looks like an object to be coveted," according to Strayhorn's biographer; "because of her high, sculpted cheekbones and flowing, waved shoulder-length hair, she resembled Marlene Dietrich, and like her, she would never stand or sit—she would lounge," characteristically with Dom Perignon in hand.

Billy Strayhorn became quite intimate with Marian, part of her inner circle, and the nucleus of regular Saturday social gatherings. He'd call from Macy's basement which sold imported foods and gourmet specialties, and bring over bags of groceries; Billy would then cook all afternoon while groups of friends—including the Copasetics, Luther Henderson, the Robinsons—would know to drop by for one of Strayhorn's legendary dinners. Afterwards, Billy usually played classical music and he and Marian talked incessantly into the night; five or six in the morning was Strayhorn's favorite time—he called it "halfway to dawn."

Sometimes the trio would take Saturday drives into the Catskills instead, with Arthur Logan behind the wheel of his sleek, immense black Impala convertible. Marian would doze and chat, while Billy reclined in the back seat, reading a book; he also brought along a portable bar. "Arthur would be looking at the countryside," Marian reported, "and say, 'Strays, there's a beautiful farmhouse' or whatever. Strays would say, 'Wonderful, Arturo, wonderful! Describe it to me.' And he'd keep reading and sipping his cocktail."

Billy Strayhorn had a reputation for acute political awareness among his friends and in jazz quarters. "Strayhorn was ahead of me in terms of what he knew—how the white world operated, who had the power, how they used it," said Dick Gregory, the comedian and activist who performed at the annual Copasetics shows in the early 1960s. Strayhorn and

Martin Luther King, Jr. were often sequestered in the Logans' kitchen for long, intense discussions. Strayhorn supported Marian's decision to help King integrate a hotel in Atlanta, and he also accompanied Lena Horne on a trip to Jackson, Mississippi in 1963 where the NAACP was preparing to stage its largest rally to date, in defiance of a state court injunction barring racial protests.

Derided by some black activists for her "white" appearance and dormancy in the early years of the civil rights movement, Lena Horne recovered self-confidence through Strayhorn's empathy. ("He was marvelous. He was there as my backbone.") In Jackson, the pair was graciously met by field representative Medgar Evers, who regretted that he couldn't invite them to stay at his home since it had recently been firebombed. Evers asked Lena Horne to perform at the upcoming rally; Strayhorn taught her "Amazing Grace" and how to sing it a cappella. Five days later, Medgar was shot in the back and killed by a white man who had been spotted at the rally. Lena Horne heard about it while she was having her makeup applied moments before an appearance on the *Today* show: unbridled, she revealed her rage on the air, live.

Strayhorn was instrumental in introducing Martin Luther King, Jr. to Duke Ellington. Arriving in Washington two days before the historic 1963 March to offer help in the preparations, Strayhorn stayed with the Logans at the Willard Hotel, where SCLC had reserved a block of rooms for King and his friends. "Strays spent most of his time in our room," said Marian Logan, "because we decided we would be the room with the booze." He "talked Martin's ear off" about his current collaboration with Ellington, "My People," an original stage production commissioned as a demonstration of black pride at an exhibition entitled "Century of Negro Progress" at Chicago's McCormick Place convention center. "Martin promised to go see it," Marian reports; later the Logans took him, "where he met Edward for the first time. They saw each other and hugged like they were old friends."

In at least one instance, Bayard Rustin and Marian Logan were allied in opposition to King's policies: both expressed doubts about the Poor People's Campaign which King proposed near the end of his life. (So did

Jesse Jackson, which prompted King to wonder if Jackson was competing with him for leadership of the SCLC.) When King sought Rustin's "strategic thinking" on this campaign, Rustin's memorandum didn't exactly oppose the project, but it raised serious reservations: the announced demands of the campaign were too broad to be achievable; a massive disruption of Washington at that time might lead to further backlash and repression; they might "not only fail to attract persons dedicated to nonviolence but also attract elements that cannot be controlled." Still on the Board of SCLC, Marian urged the cancellation of the Poor People's Campaign. King was deeply wounded by her letter, partly because he discerned the influence of Rustin, whom he knew was a close friend of the Logans.

Strayhorn and Rustin had a lot more in common than simply a circle of prominent friends, or even their own lifelong, self-styled cosmopolitanism. Both had the advantage of attending excellent, integrated public high schools in Pennsylvania (Strayhorn went to Westinghouse High, endowed by George Westinghouse) from which they emerged with polished skills (particularly musical) that enabled them, unlike most of their peers, to move to New York. By the time Rustin graduated valedictorian from West Chester High, as an all around athlete, musician and scholar, he was leading sit-in demonstrations against segregated movie theaters, soda fountains, department stores and the YMCA, racking up the first of his 25 lifetime arrests. (Although West Chester, a Quaker stronghold, had been an important stop on the underground railroad, not even the local NAACP had ever been willing to be this confrontational.) At Rustin's instigation, his fellow black football players refused to participate in a game with a neighboring school until they were pulled out of their Jim Crow accommodations and housed with the rest of the team.

As a young man, Billy Strayhorn was a prominent figure in Pittsburgh's music scene; a bit of a loner and a brilliant classical pianist, thought of as a genius by his classmates, Billy began playing piano at house parties of his wealthier peers. He was soon working with local ensembles and jazz bands at black clubs downtown, and then with the integrated Rex Edwards Orchestra. Strayhorn's chief influences were Art Tatum and

Teddy Wilson (both black) and Benny Goodman to whom he'd listen for many hours on the radio. In high school, Strayhorn was composing and staging sophisticated orchestral works, such as "Fantastic Rhythm" which was so successful that it was booked into the Roosevelt Theater, Pittsburgh's most prestigious black venue. He performed his composition "Concerto for Piano and Percussion" at his graduation—years later, some fellow students thought they remembered him playing Gershwin's "Rhapsody in Blue" there, another major influence—after which Strayhorn briefly attended the Pittsburgh Musical Institute. Yearning for an urbane lifestyle as well as for the music scene in New York, Strayhorn subscribed to the *New Yorker*, and composed songs such as "Lush Life" which his biographer describes as a "masterpiece of fatalist sophistication that belies its author's youth but betrays years of ferment."

Billy and Bayard were born within 2 years of each other, and have somewhat similar familial backgrounds, especially supportive mothers and grandmothers with whom they were very close. Both of the Strayhorns' parents' families were middle class, but his father could only find manual labor and began drinking heavily. To protect Billy from an abusive father and older brother, his mother, Lillian, who'd been educated at Shaw College, started sending her son to spend summers in Hillsborough, N.C. at his grandmother's spacious, airy house surrounded by beautiful flower beds. (There, Strayhorn's lifelong passion for flowers developed, which he shared with intimates like Lena Horne and Marian Logan. Billy made it a habit to bring Marian Logan one white flower, of any variety, every time he saw her.) His grandmother was the pianist for church, and with her encouragement, he taught himself to play spirituals on her piano, picking out melodies. By the time Billy returned home, piano was his complete focus, and the 11-year-old quickly set about to earn enough money to buy one, selling newspapers and working as a drugstore delivery boy. After that, his pay went for sheet music, and to finance his own lessons from Charlotte Catlin, a black woman associated with a music store that was the hub of musical Pittsburgh.

Bayard came from a more privileged background: the Rustins were one of the few prominent, black Quaker families in eastern Pennsylvania. At age 11, Rustin discovered that Julia Ralston whom he believed to be his mother was actually his grandmother: one of her 6 teenage daughters (Bayard was raised as their brother) had a child out of wedlock and basically left Julia to raise him. Bayard always regarded her as his mother, and scarcely ever saw his biological parents. A former nurse and civic activist, Julia helped found organizations like the Garden Club and the Community Center—established for the nonwhites who were barred from the YMCA/YWCA. As there were no black guesthouses in West Chester, she often hosted such visiting leaders as W.E.B. Dubois and James Weldon Johnson. Her husband was an accomplished caterer for the Elks Club and for a number of wealthy families. Although Julia frequently invited Bayard's white friends to their home, this gesture was never reciprocated despite his unusual popularity: that only furthered Rustin's determination to stage a series of local protests.

Bayard Rustin and Billy Strayhorn both moved to Harlem in the late 1930s, and quickly took up with intellectual and artistic circles, mostly of gay black men. Mercer Ellington soon introduced Billy to Aaron Bridgers, another black pianist and recent refugee from the South. The two were immediately inseparable. "We had everything in common, particularly music. We became very close right away," explained Bridgers who was working an elevator in a Lexington Avenue hotel while studying informally with jazz virtuoso Art Tatum. Francophiles, Billy and Bridgers went out every night to different ethnic restaurants, gabbing away in French on the subway. Before the end of the year, they moved in together. With the help of Bridgers' hotel coworkers, part of their basement space was rebuilt as a young cosmopolitan's dream pad. They had a long bar constructed in the living room with a row of tube-steel stools with red leather cushions. To complete their cocktail lounge ambience, they also arranged a couple of round bar tables and chairs in the center of the room and brought in an upright piano, a long couch and some Matisse prints.

Billy could work no matter what was going on around him, having conditioned himself to block out his family's household distractions: Bridgers might be composing at the same time or listening to his favorite records, Bartok and Hindeminth. The couple frequented Café Society, which had both uptown and downtown branches featuring gifted young black performers like Hazel Scott and Sarah Vaughan, where they always felt entirely welcome. In 1951, though, Bridgers moved to Paris to become house pianist at the Mars Club, an international gay watering hole. Billy visited Aaron several times; remaining intimate, their relationship was basically over. For a while toward the end of his life, Billy lived with, and became deeply dependent on Francis Goldberg, a good looking, retired black sailor. Both men were drinking night and day, and Goldberg was very controlling, destructive and jealous of Billy's friends. When he accompanied Billy to the Logans' buffets, for instance, Goldberg would station himself at the head of the table and wait to be served. "Anybody joke around with him and say something anywhere teasing, Goldie went into a fit," reported Marian Logan. "'How *dare* you talk to me that way?'"

Less seems to be known about Rustin, or at least his biographer has chosen to say little on the subject of his sexuality. Though certainly never in the closet to friends and colleagues, when Rustin was arrested in the Los Angeles scandal, and his sexuality became public knowledge, he was perceived by some as compromising his political effectiveness: he suffered considerably by losing the support of his beloved mentor, A.J. Muste. Rustin has stated that when he first became aware of his homosexuality as an adolescent, he discussed with his mother "'going to parties with boys for purposes of dating.' Her reply was 'Then I suppose that's what you need to do.' It wasn't an encouragement, but it was a recognition." Although none of his high school friends were aware of his homosexuality, Rustin claimed he never had to pretend, and never experienced feelings of guilt.

The young Bayard was a handsome and compelling figure, and apparently quite active sexually and romantically. He went off to Wilberforce College briefly (W.E.B. Dubois' first job was teaching language there, which he quit when they wouldn't let him establish a sociology department), but Rustin left school after a year: it was rumored that he had fallen in love with the president's son. The following year, he enrolled in Cheyney State Teacher's College, a local black school founded by Philadelphia Quakers, until he was booted out in less than two years for reasons which remain unspecified in the book. Rustin himself admitted later that he had been "naughty" and "misbehaved," and "in a moment of youthful carelessness he had made a mistake."

What P B-R found most lacking in Jervis Anderson's otherwise admirable biography is almost all information about Rustin's longtime companions, and any sense of how successful he was in defeating the overwhelming homophobia of the times to create intimate, meaningful relationships. Readily admitting to a somewhat morbid curiosity about partisan politics, why the left could never get together (and why the international CP was so eager to accept orders from Russia's "central committee"), it was really the question of what kinds of relationships Rustin was able to establish within such a repressive milieu that was at the heart of P B-R's interest. This absence is particularly notable when Anderson mentions in passing that during the last 12 years of his life, Bayard settled permanently with Charles Naegle, about whom we learn very little (not even his ethnicity), except that he accompanied Rustin on several trips to Africa and Europe, and they were together when Bayard died.

Even more bizarre, other sources report that Tom Kahn was also Bayard's lover—Kahn and Rochelle Horowitz were Rustin's protégés and longtime assistants in numerous pacifist and civil rights organizations and struggles (Michael Harrington referred to them as "Bayard Rustin's Marching and Chowder Society"). Maurice Isserman's biography of Harrington contains one footnoted sentence to this effect: in context of discussing sectarian fights, and Rustin allies Kahn and Horowitz, he says, "That Rustin and Tom Kahn soon became lovers helped cement the political alliance between them." This doesn't enter into the Jervis account at all, which only describes Kahn as Bayard's "close friend and intellectual aide."

Of course, it's pointless to compare people's lives, especially in terms of happiness, or self-esteem, though if P B-R were here (instead of in Florida, ensconced in *The Charterhouse of Parma* for the duration of the parental visit), he'd doubtlessly be doing just that. In this case, the need seems so compelling: trying to understand how 2 publicly "out" gay black men coped in a time when they didn't even have legal rights; what types of self-images and complex feelings could they possibly have experienced? Both men appear to have been highly respected in the internationally accomplished circles of which they were integral parts. On the other hand, Billy Strayhorn did basically drink himself to death at age 51; he also had cancer of the esophagus, and at the end he was pouring martinis into a shunt in his stomach.

Bayard Rustin lived till he was 75, when over 1,000 of his friends, acquaintances and admirers gathered for a memorial service at Manhattan's Community Church. Certainly, his fierce commitment to both the international peace movement and fighting racism had been established beyond dispute by many arrests, beatings, a chain gang, and penitentiary which he endured over the years. But Rustin was also much vilified in the latter decades of his life by quite a few former friends and staunchest allies. In regard to happiness, everyone who ever heard Rustin sing "Sometimes I Feel Like a Motherless Chile" reports that it was a very moving experience. (When the actress Liv Ullman first heard him, in her later years, she remarked, "I didn't find it like singing. It was more like crying out—Listen, listen to my sadness—like a sharing of the spirit.")

When the men were dying, both were fortunate to have friends and colleagues at hand, to die with companions, and not alone. (As the cold and brilliant light/light gradually dims, our heroes emerge into the foreground, shadowy but somehow exuding a promise of pristine and clear visibility to come; the unearthly producer, the set-designer and the lighting specialist must see to that.) The winter after he was diagnosed with cancer, Strayhorn began developing a close relationship with an acquaintance of Frank Neal's from his days at the Chicago Art Institute: Bill Grove was 2 years younger than Billy, a graphic designer and art director of the magazine *Consumer Reports*, who had studied watercolor painting as a boy. Grove was quiet and seemed expressionless, and had socialized primarily with black men his whole life. Marian Logan says, "Strays found just what he needed right then with Grove. They both drank like it was water, but they talked a lot and Grove listened to Strays. He was a listener. Goldie was a talker. They went to movies. They read magazines and books." Often, renting a limousine, they'd take a ride out of Manhattan, sometimes with friends, including Grove's ex-lover, spending the day drinking and stopping along the roads in New Jersey to shop for fruits, herbs and knick knacks.

Grove never moved in but increasingly they were together all the time: over the months, a new theme emerged in Billy's apartment. Grove gave Billy an original oil painting of the sun and a ceramic serving dish glazed like the sun. A friend said, "They became enamored of the sun and its radiance and powers of life-giving." Billy held on and his friends rallied around him. Near the end, Lena Horne and her husband Lenny Hayton took the couple to Palm Springs where they had a vacation home; Billy was so weak that his friends decided to contact his family. Billy was grateful that his mother died soon afterwards and was spared the sight of his own deterioration.

Professionally, Billy's career hit a high note in his last years. His old Copasetic friend Honi Coles, among the few who knew of Strayhorn's illness, urged him to expend his creative energies more judiciously. "'I told him, Do your own stuff—write a symphony.'" Then in March, 1965, three representatives from the Duke Ellington Jazz Society offered Strayhorn the opportunity to be featured in the first solo concert of his lifetime. The committee convinced a reluctant Billy by arguing the extended-family aspect, that he'd be playing for an audience not off the street but to a community who already loved his work. He wrote new and vigorous arrangements for the whole second half of his sold-out concert at the New School auditorium, which was an enormous success both with the audience (Billy received a standing ovation when he walked on stage dolled up in a new, bright white suit) and critically.

Ellington was out of town, but when he heard about the concert, he arranged for Strayhorn and his Riverside Drive Five to record their numbers for an album which Ellington himself produced and financed. Billy continued to work on some of Ellington's more important projects including his "sacred music" which was inspired partly in reaction to his friend's mortality. Strayhorn personally participated in one of these concerts, at midnight on Christmas in the Fifth Avenue Presbyterian Church during which Lena Horne, demurely gorgeous, her hair wrapped in a white silk scarf, snuggled next to Billy on the piano bench and sang a new ballad to his plaintive piano.

Some 350 mourners came to Strayhorn's funeral services: family members, friends, admirers and colleagues like Louis Armstrong, Lena Horne, the Robinsons, Otto Preminger, Benny Goodman, Carmen McRae, Milt Jackson and Sylvia Sims. Scheduled to deliver the only eulogy, Duke Ellington had horror in his eyes and a nervous smile as he grasped the altar. He began with "Poor Little Swee' Pea, Billy Strayhorn, the biggest human being who ever lived, the most majestic artistic stature…whose impeccable tastes commanded the respect of all musicians and of all listeners." Ellington briefly enumerated Billy's superlative qualities: a rare sensitivity; honesty not only to others but to himself; unlimited patience which never involved any competitive aspirations. "He demanded freedom of expression and lived in what we consider the most important and moral of freedoms: freedom from fear, unconditionally, freedom from self-pity (even throughout all the pain and bad news) and freedom from the kind of pride that could make a man feel he was better than his brother or neighbor."

For the next few months, uncharacteristically, Ellington was deeply depressed, listless and detached. He decided to relieve his grief musically and began arrangements for an all-star concert tribute to Strayhorn at New York's Philharmonic Hall: proceeds would be donated to the Julliard School of Music as seed money for an annual scholarship in Billy Strayhorn's name. At the same time, Ellington was putting together an album of new renditions of Strayhorn and Strayhorn-Ellington compositions. Held only 3 months after Billy's death, the recording sessions at RCA records "were shaded gray by Strayhorn's shadow." ("You kept expecting to turn your head and see him," said Jimmy Hamilton.) The musicians played like it: the music was full of trenchant solos, particularly by Johnny Hodges, and was "solemn, tormented, unnervingly intimate."

It seems fitting that David Hadju titled his much welcomed study of Billy Strayhorn, *Lush Life*. Begun some years earlier, this signature song of his youth was published in 1936 when Billy was 21. Hadju terms it "a prayer," and calls it a "masterpiece of ferment." He notes that the work exquisitely weds words and music: "a key change on 'everything seemed so sure' suddenly suggests options, and stress notes, for instance the blue E-natural on the word 'jazz' fell precisely on the lyric's point of drama." Billy himself was clearly attached to his composition. When he was first becoming intimate with Lena Horne, they talked and he played "Lush Life" all night long: she reported falling in love with him then. Strayhorn avoided recording "Lush Life" and was furious at Nat "King" Cole's rendition. Aaron Bridgers says, "When he first heard Nat's 'Lush Life,' that was the only time I ever, ever heard Billy really upset."

The lyrics of this lovely and melancholic song are:

> *I used to visit all the very gay places,*
> *Those come what may places*
> *Where one relaxes on the axis*
> *Of the wheel of life*
> *To get the feel of life*
> *From jazz and cocktails.*
>
> *The girls I knew had sad and sullen gray faces*
> *With distingué traces*
> *That used to be there, you could see where*
> *They'd been washed away*
> *By too many through the day*
> *Twelve o'clock tales.*
>
> *Then you came along with your siren song*
> *To tempt me to madness.*
> *I thought for a while that your poignant smile*
> *Was tinged with the sadness of a great love for me.*
> *Ah, yes, I was wrong,*
> *Again I was wrong.*
>
> *Life is lonely again*
> *And only last year*
> *Everything seemed so sure.*

Now life is awful again,
A trough full of heart
Could only be a bore.

A week in Paris will ease the bite of it.
All I care is to smile in spite of it.
I'll forget you, I will
While yet you are still
Burning inside my brain.

Romance is mush
Stifling those who strive.
I'll live a lush life in some small dive
And there I'll be while I rot with the rest
Of those whose lives are lonely, too.

"Lush Life" seems like the ballad, or anthem, for Billy's generation of gay people, as well as for those who came after, especially those who refused to be dispossessed: despite the crushing loneliness, fighting against what they fully recognized as monstrous obstacles, yearning for love.

MEL FREILICHER is a longtime San Diego resident who was publisher and co-editor of *CRAWL OUT YOUR WINDOW* for 15 years, a magazine of regional literature and arts; he was an activist, including working with downtown artists' groups; did a stint as a performance artist, and was the first Vice-President of the Board of Sushi. Freilicher has been anthologized in Sun and Moon press' *Contemporary American Fiction*, and has chapbooks out from Standing Stones Press and Obscure publications. His reviews, essays, and fiction have appeared in many publications, such as *American Book Review, Central Park, Fiction International, San Diego Free Press, San Diego Union-Tribune, Flue: Magazine of Franklin Furnace Archive, NY; Frame-work: Journal of the LA Center for Photographic Studies; San Diego Reader, River Styx, Fourteen Hills, Golden Handcuffs Review, eye-rhyme: journal of experimental literature*. Freilicher has been teaching literature and writing at UCSD and SDSU for several decades.

Photo: Joe Keenan